Shades of Jane

Footprints of Love

G. A. BECKETT

SHADES OF JANE (Footprints of Love)

First published June 2024
ISBN: 978-0-6458689-9-9 Paperback
ISBN: 978-0-9756379-0-6 E-Book

DISCLAIMER

This book is memoir. It reflects the author's present recollections of experiences over time. Some names and characteristics have been changed, some events have been compressed, and some dialogue has been recreated. This is a work of fiction. Although its form is that of an autobiography, it is not one. Space and time have been rearranged to suit the convenience of the book, and with the exception of public figures, any resemblance of persons living or dead is coincidental. The opinions expressed are those of the characters and should not be confused with the author.

Contents

Introduction v

The First Encounter 1

Meet the Parents. 7

Singapore and Concerts 13

Bangkok and Pattaya Thailand. 23

Phuket Thailand 33

Hong Kong. 43

Shenzhen and Taiwan.. 51

Japan. 55

Las Vegas (Our Wedding). 61

Hawaii. 71

L.A and San Diego. 79

Queen Mary and Baja California 87

San Francisco 91

New York.. 95

New Orleans. 99

Miami and The Caribbean. 105

Canada and Seattle. 109

London England. 115

Paris and Cannes, France.. 121

Amsterdam and Barcelona. 127

Rome and Berlin. 133

Copenhagen, Norway, Sweden & The Baltic Cruise. .139

Moscow.. 147

The Philippines.. 155

The Pregnancy. 165

Ho Chi Minh, Vietnam.. 171

Da Nang and Hanoi, Vietnam. 179

Cambodia and Bali.. 183

Gemelu .189

The Final Twist 195

Introduction

Life has a way of testing even the strongest of bonds. Challenges will emerge, obstacles that were not anticipated. Doubts would creep into our minds, threatening to overshadow the love we hold so dear. It is in those moments that we will truly understand the depth of attraction. This is a tale of a love that defies time and the challenges that life presents. It will remind us that when two souls are meant to be, no obstacle is too significant to conquer.

Marking the genesis of my rebirth, the power to redefine who I was and aspired to be, I vowed to welcome this fresh beginning and shed the weight of my tumultuous past. The echoes of my regrets dissolved, and I could feel the universe conspiring in my favor, whispering tales of uncharted territories.

I know that destiny had crafted a thrilling surprise, beckoning me toward an extraordinary encounter that would change the very fabric of my existence. With newfound clarity, I realized that this extraordinary encounter was no mere coincidence. I abandoned the remnants of my former self and embraced the boundless potential of the unknown. Navigating life's twists and turns with unwavering determination for the transformative power of second chances. I decided to forget my past before this amazing day and cherish my new beginning.

In a world woven with words and ink, my quill danced across the page, leaving behind trails of stories that would captivate hearts and minds alike. With every stroke, I seek not only to entertain but to inspire and ignite the dormant minds. With every word I now write, I aspire to encourage others, spark their imaginations, and remind them that within each ending, lays the potential for a breathtaking new beginning. Most normal people will say I am suffering from delusion, and in the mainstream way of thinking, most would agree. After all, the thoughts in my exposed mind were bordering on insanity in the true essence of thinking, but I had a secret that was real. This secret would push me to speed up my future decisions.

Chapter 1

The First Encounter

October 20, 2010, the date my life began, not to be confused with my birthdate, which incidentally is October 1, 1959. I was moving on from a somewhat shaky past and the new surprising episodes in my life, you could say it took courage, but I just left behind my regrets, failures and heartaches. On this fateful day, something extraordinary happened that would change my perspective on life forever. This phenomenon was the dawning of time in my universe with a feeling of hope, and my aspirations were in a good place.

Walking aimlessly in the city streets, feeling lost and unsure of myself about the true answer to life, I found my destiny, and I recall being married to this unique woman that I was now looking at in amazement. As fate would have it, I now found my past life clashed with my present. I arrived back in this life in a different place, and I now mysteriously discovered my destiny. I shared my past life with this woman named Jane. It was a love story that transcended time, defying the limitations of logic and reason.

Fate seemed to have conspired to bring her back to me once more. My heart gravitated towards this woman, and it was uncanny the resemblance of my past wife was to my present vision. Her smile was more natural, and it glowed on the water and performed a show for my eyes to view vividly, and my imagination was now reality. I felt I had the ability, or as some would interpret, a gift that allowed me to see visions of the past. I never shared this secret with others as they would have me put away, or certainly no one would believe me.

While strolling along Orchard Road, I stumbled upon a small shop called Perfect Potion. This shop sold products to enhance the beauty of both men and women, all made from natural sources. I was intrigued by the mystic aura that seemed to force me to enter. Immediately, I noticed Jane with her sparkling eyes and gentle, soft demeanor. I was captivated by her grace and kind, alluring smile. At this moment, I heard a clear voice that echoed the words, "You will marry this woman and spend your life with her." I felt a delicate balance between sanity and madness. Ignoring this mystery voice, as strange as it might sound, I thought, "What if the mystery voice was right?". I then felt boldness I had never felt before, which gave me the courage to invite her to Starbucks after her work. Judging by the warm smile that lit up her angelic face, she seemed happy at my invitation. I was delighted that Jane accepted, and little did she know I saw flashes of our past life together.

Now we both sat drinking tea and holding hands like we had never parted for one hundred and fifty years. I did not share my physic vision and our past life with this girl as this may have scared my angel away. I found myself time-traveling back to the past century when I had first encountered Jane. Back then, we had shared fleeting moments over cups of steaming coffee amidst the aroma of freshly brewed beans. But circumstances had torn us apart, leaving a lingering ache that transcended lifetimes.

In this new existence, the present Jane mirrored the essence of her past self. Her eyes sparkled with the same warmth, and her laughter rang with the same enchanting melody. Now, as we reconnected, the memories flooded back, intertwined dreams of the past with the reality of the present. Our love story became a dance between two worlds. I longed to share the secrets of our previous life to unveil the intricacies of our timeless connection. As our bond deepened, my experiences and thoughts drifted between the realms of reality and dreams. They spoke of forgotten memories, of stolen moments from another era. Jane and I discovered the power of our connection. It was a love that surpassed logic and reason, a force that spanned centuries.

Holding hands while talking sweet and soft, I noticed in the distance little arrows from the bow of Cupid coming in my direction and penetrating my heart. I did not mind too much, and the sharp pain was bearable. After all, we loved before and now love again. Jane's eyes twinkled with delight as I lavished her with attention and felt her comfort in our connection, growing stronger with each passing minute. As Forrest Gump once said, "We were like peas and carrots. "It seemed evident that fate had brought us together once again for a reason.

I invited Jane to spend the night with me, and we kissed passionately once inside the room. My heart was beating louder than a native drum beating out a message to a nearby village, and the message was love. Within the confines of that room, time seemed to stand still. The outside world faded away, leaving only the two of us in a cocoon of bliss. It was as if a dream I never dared to believe in was becoming a reality before my eyes.

The night unfolded like a symphony of passion and tenderness. Our bodies together, each movement in perfect harmony. In that space of absolute contentment, our souls merged into one. As the night gave way to dawn, we clung to each other, reluctant to let go. We both knew that this was just the beginning of a beautiful journey. Our reunion had ignited our past flame that would guide us through the obstacles that lay ahead. We had a lovely night of bliss where time stood still together in my small, humble hotel room, a dream that was becoming true, and the feeling of absolute contentment engulfed my willing body. I felt even the universe was celebrating our reunion.

The following day, the sun brought a bittersweet reality. I longed to spend more time wrapped in my angel's loving embrace, but she had responsibilities, so we had to move as Jane had to be at work that day. When she departed for work, I had a heavy heart as I watched her leave.

Maybe I was presumptuous or crazy, but I wanted to finalize our bond, and tonight, all this would be answered by how Jane would react to questions based on love and a promise of total commitment. I spent my day searching for the perfect engagement ring. I wanted to show Jane my commitment, to promise her a lifetime of love and happiness. The anticipation filled my every step as I imagined her reaction to my grand gesture of devotion.

As the evening arrived and the clock reached 7 p.m. I sauntered, contemplating what I had done, and I heard my inner mind speaking, saying, "Geoff, are you there?" trying to persuade me to wake up. I finally arrived at Perfect Potion, the shop where Jane works and the same place where we first met and waited for her to finish work. As Jane came out of the shop, our eyes locked, and love radiated between them. She noticed me smiling in a way filled with admiration for her beauty. Jane's face lit up when she was close and hugged me tight and kissed my lips in a sweet way that made me realize this was right and that there were no more doubts.

We had a simple dinner and went back to my hotel called Robinson Quay Hotel, a short walk from Clarke Quay, which was one of the popular locations for tourists in Singapore. Once inside the room, with trembling hands, I sat Jane on the bed and got down on my knee. I presented the ring and asked her to commit her life to me and be engaged to me, and one day, when the time was right, be married to me. The air became still as Jane's eyes widened; her emotions uncontained.

If you think about the craziness of asking this girl to marry me, whom I only knew for two days, I felt it was the right time. I knew this angel from my past life, where the lines of time and fate connected. I know to most people, this would never be understood, and they would just think I was insane; I knew our tale of love defied logic and reason.

Jane smiled and said, "Yes! I love you, Geoff," with a voice of excitement and disbelief. Tears swelled in her eyes, overflowing with happiness, and she confirmed without further words our inexplicit bond. I could see a thrilled girl who showered me with kisses; our love would be shared in the chronicles. We made beautiful love to seal the commitment without boundaries or rules, falling asleep with our bodies entwined. Our story was unconventional, with the power of love's undeniable force as the ultimate winner.

Morning arrived, and I was awoken by birds singing or more like parrots squawking in abundance in the outside trees. Their squawks reverberated through the room, a lively and unexpected alarm clock. Blinking my eyes open, my mind and brain slowly woke up, and I sighed with relief as I realized it was not a dream. There beside me lay the love of my life, her pretty face adorned with a simple beauty. Her embrace was both comforting and energizing.

I seized the magic, and I found comfort as I gazed upon the peacefully sleeping form of my fiancé. I marveled at the gift of this present moment. The symphony of parrots outside served as a joyful reminder that life's surprises can awaken us from our slumbers, reminding us to appreciate every breath and every heartbeat.

What would lay ahead would need to be seen for Jane and me with unimaginable travel adventures in the coming years of my life no one could believe. In this time, our open minds and boundless imagination would explore the realms no other mortals could even fathom. We lived like no one could dream, pushing the boundaries of what was deemed possible. This tale will remind us that love is not bound by the constraints of time or space. It exists beyond the tangible. And though the complexities of such love may bewilder the mind, I accepted the magic of its existence. For in the realm where dreams are combined with reality, anything is possible, even the eternal reunion of two souls destined to be together.

We had now chosen to embark on a journey together. It was a commitment made not only for the fleeting moments of this earthly existence but for the infinite years that awaited us. The passing of time seemed inconsequential. We would navigate the highs and lows as the world continued to spin around us. Eternity, as elusive and mysterious as it may be, would find its place in our shared reality. Jane and I would now live as one for eternity or whatever years I had left on this planet we call Earth.

Chapter 2

Meet the Parents.

The next important thing we had to do was tell Jane's mum and dad we were engaged, and she would be leaving work to spend her life with me. I understood the worries they might have, for I was a few years older than their daughter and came from a world they were not familiar with. I had an idea what they would say as, in reality, I am just a total stranger. I also know they have other plans for her life.

I felt it was the right thing to show courtesy and inform them of their daughter's decision to be with me. I did not expect their approval, but in time, I hoped they would see it was the correct one. I intended to give Jane all my love and care and try to make all her dreams come true, which would be easy as I was pure of heart and soul.

Her dad lived in Singapore, and her mother was not here this time, so Jane told her mother to fly to Singapore as she had something significant to share with her and her dad. I insisted on buying her mother's air ticket, and within the week, she was arriving in Singapore. She must have wondered why Jane insisted on buying her ticket to come to Singapore as this was very unusual.

Jane's mother couldn't help but feel a mix of confusion and frustration as she questioned Jane why she had not come home for over one week. She was puzzled to the point of anger, but our secret was held tight in our lips, not to be told to them or mentioned. Her mum demanded to know what the urgent news was, but we both kept tight-lipped and prepared to face them with the news as we thought this was the best way. I would not anticipate their reaction and would let it flow and see the result. I made a reservation for lunch for Saturday at the Marriott Hotel in Orchard Road as that day, they served a magnificent seafood buffet just a few days after her anticipated arrival.

Saturday arrived without any hold-ups, as most Saturdays arrived after Friday, and this week was without exception. Walking into the restaurant at the Marriott, we were surprised to see the parents waiting as they arrived early and looked so confused to see me and Jane smiling and holding hands. The puzzle pieces began to fall into place for Jane's parents as they realized the valid reason for their daughter's urgency. I introduced myself, and they seemed okay at this moment. "My name is Geoff." I shook the father's hand, which had a firm grip, indicating they were solid and hard-working hands, but his face seemed kind and gentle. He then replied and softly said, "My name is Gomez." Her father, usually calm and composed, wore a stern expression.

I knew that breaking this news would not be easy. Jane's mother looked at us with a mix of anticipation and concern. At this point, I was relieved the mother's name was not Morticia when she introduced herself, and in a strict voice, she said, "My name is Meredith". I was thinking about the crazy '60s comedy show "The Adams Family". I am confident no person would marry into that family, no matter how many arrows of Cupid were embedded deep within the heart. The mother seemed a tough lady and looked at me with total disapproval, but to her credit, she was friendly and polite. Her eyes were a different story, so we all sat and prepared to give the news.

I was chosen as the spokesman, and before talking, I held up Jane's hand, showed the diamond ring to the parents, and said, "Jane and I have something important to share with you." Silence hung heavily for a moment before Jane spoke up, her voice steady but laced with emotion. "We are engaged!" Jane said out of turn, but it was good she broke the ice. And I said, "Yes, we are engaged, and one day I will marry her, and Jane will leave Singapore and her work and be always with me." I pushed the words out quickly, and what I said gave the complete picture, as no other meaning could be taken from my honest words.

The mother was so shocked and said, "What a joke! You only knew each other for just over a week and now become engaged after knowing each other for two days?". I felt the information about our past life was better kept secret, or the upset mother would then have thought I was off my rocker. There was a moment of silence as her parent exchanged glances, their eyes revealing a mix of surprise and concern. But then, unexpectedly, a smile crept onto the face of Gomez. It was a moment frozen in time, where opposing worlds collided, each carrying its own set of expectations and prejudices.

Gomez studied me for a brief moment, his eyes assessing me as I stood before him. He could see the love reflected in my eyes as he looked at Jane. It was a genuine love, unmarred by the judgment of others. He spoke with his warm and kind voice but with a hint of skepticism. "Young man, love knows no boundaries, and we can see the depth of your affection for our daughter. If Jane has found happiness with you, then who are we to stand in the way?". His words were a huge relief to hear, and I felt he was genuine, but I could feel total disapproval from the mother as she remained silent.

So here we were, all nervously eating our lunch and talking small talk, as I did not want to make this lunch full of deep discussion and heavy emotions. After all, I did not know their likes or dislikes, political or religious views on the world. From time to time, I left them alone with Jane as I excused myself and gathered some food, and as I glanced from a distance, I could see intense talking between the three of them. I could only imagine what was said, but Jane did not faultier her promise to me. Her commitment was strong, and Jane simply said to her parents, "All is final, and Geoff is my destiny."

Our love story would continue to unfold. For we discovered that even in the most unexpected circumstances, love has the power to bridge differences, ignite hearts, and create a tapestry of endless love and togetherness. As the lunch came to an end, I couldn't help but feel a wave of relief wash over my entire body. The tension that had filled the air during the conversation slowly dissipated, leaving behind a sense of peace. Jane excused herself and accompanied her parents back to their home to gather her belongings.

I was resolute in my choice. Despite the confusion that occasionally crept into my mind, I never once doubted my love for Jane. I believed deep in my heart that she was my soul mate, the one I had been searching for all my life. I always had a vision I would find my past wife; even before I met her in Singapore, I knew she was back in this world waiting for me to capture her again. Jane worked hard for the past six years in Singapore, six to seven days per week, and half that time, she worked as a nurse, which was her career before she left the hospital for a career change to work in Perfect Potion.

As I awaited Jane's return, I felt a mix of anticipation and anxiety. I knew that embarking on this new Journey together would not be without its challenges, but I was ready to face them head-on. Love had a way of defying logic and transforming lives, and I was willing to take that leap of faith.

Paranoia crept inside my head the few hours we were apart, and I knew full well that the mum and dad would have attempted to bring her to her senses. I knew that Jane's parents, more likely the mother, would try to sway her decision. They were probably grappling with the sudden change in their daughter's life, struggling to understand her newfound love and commitment. This sudden change in the direction of their daughter's life would take time for them to understand. Even in love, I was confused, but never once did I rethink my decision. I was sure Jane was the one and would always be the one that I desired to be with from this day forward.

As Jane walked through the door, the clock on the wall chimed 8 p.m. Only one suitcase accompanied her, maybe containing all her worldly possessions. We didn't bother opening it, instead opting for passionate kisses filled with anticipation and excited chatter about our future together. Jane shared that her parents disapproved of our relationship, but at that moment, her words resonated deeply within me. She told them defiantly, "Approve or not, I love Geoff, and I will marry him. I want to be with him forever". Hearing those resolute words from my beloved's lips brought such comfort to my soul.

With exhaustion tugging at our bodies from the emotional rollercoaster of the day, we found solace in each other's arms. Wrapped tightly together, we drifted off to sleep. That night, my dreams were vivid, bathed in clarity. I found contentment in the beauty of the present moment.

A vision of Aphrodite, the mythological Greek goddess of love, was the leading player in my dream, a true sign that encouraged my emotions to keep loving Jane more robust and much more.

Chapter 3

Singapore and Concerts

I awoke on Sunday morning after a sleep filled with amazing dreams that took me back to the times of ancient rulers in distant lands, and because of these vivid dreams and the anticipation of my future life with Jane, my face felt stretched from smiling while asleep. As we finished our breakfast, Jane and I looked at each other, our hearts filled with excitement. Realizing one job was left to do before we would be free.

Tomorrow would mark a significant step forward to the life we had always dreamed of. Jane would give her boss one month's notice that she was leaving work. We discussed our plans for the future; Jane would leave her job to begin a new chapter of her life with her destiny filled with love and happiness. Her decision to quit work was not taken lightly, as it meant leaving behind her familiarity and security.

Monday morning dawned, and the world continued its ceaseless spin while my love for Jane only grew stronger with each passing day. As I dropped her off at her workplace, a surge of separation anxiety overwhelmed me, making it difficult to let go. I couldn't help but notice her boss's disapproving gaze fixed upon us, her eyes holding an intensity that sent shivers down my spine. It was as if she saw me not as a human being but as a creature to be scorned.

Nonetheless, I brushed off the unsettling encounter, thinking to myself, "Wait until she hears the news today." Perhaps she possessed some innate psychic ability, leading her to anticipate the impending revelation. The look on her face, reminiscent of the sorrowful frown of someone recovering from a painful breakup, could only be explained by her premonition of what was to come. Little did her boss know that the moment marked the beginning of a new chapter in our lives.

That evening, I returned to pick up Jane from work, and her boss was very upset that she was leaving her job in one month. She quickly exited the shop and began hurling insults and trying to convince Jane that I was not worthy of her love.

Jane's boss, fueled by a deep-seated resentment, aimed to undermine the love and connection we shared. In her eyes, I was unworthy of Jane's affections, and she accused me of merely toying with her emotions. She painted a picture of me as a controlling figure, convinced that true happiness lies within the confines of their workplace. This Chinese Singaporean lady had no right to interfere in our relationship, to claim that my love for Jane was false. How could she presume to know our hearts? What knowledge of life did she possess that gave her the authority to pass judgment? I chose not to stoop to her level, not to judge her in return. Instead, I recognized that her negativity reflected a soul devoid of contentment. Her attempts to break us apart stemmed from her discontentment with life.

As her boss urged me to leave and never return to Singapore, I stood my ground. She seemed to think her words bothered me, but in reality, they just flew directly over my head and crashed into the wall behind me. The harsh words she spat were nothing more than empty noise. I chose silence as my weapon, understanding that it held greater strength. By refusing to engage in her toxic game, I retained control over my emotions and preserved the purity of my intentions.

I was trying to maintain my composure in the face of such hostility. Though the boss's words stung, I reminded myself that I knew the truth and that Jane and I shared something special. For love thrives in the face of adversity. It is not swayed by the disapproval of others or the harsh words they may hurl. Love, when nurtured with care and tenderness, becomes an unbreakable force capable of weathering any storm.

Setting aside the insults hurled at me, I turned to Jane, determined to shield her from this hostile environment. I reached out and gently clasped her hand, reassuring her that none of the accusations held any truth. The weight of her boss's words began to dissipate as Jane's eyes sparkled with gratitude and relief. Together, we walked away from that place, leaving behind the darkness and negativity. No external force could shake the foundation of our love, for it was built on a deep understanding and unwavering commitment. As we moved forward, I vowed to protect Jane from the judgment and doubt that others may cast upon us. Our journey would be marked by resilience and a refusal to let the opinions of others define our happiness. We would travel on a path that was uniquely ours, where love blossomed in the face of adversity.

As we left this hostile environment behind, we embraced the freedom to write our own story, guided by the boundless power of our love. Soon, we were in a taxi, and Jane seemed confused when I told the driver, "Marina Bay Sands, please, Sir." Once we were on our way, I felt the time was right, so I surprised Jane by pulling two tickets to a stage show from my pocket. "Honey, we are going to see Jersey Boys". I could see by my darling's face she was totally at a loss to know what I meant. I explained this was a stage show that traced the life of a '60s group called the Four Seasons and the lead singer, Frankie Valli.

The show started at 8 p.m., so we only had time for a quick snack washed down with a Tiger beer, the local Singapore beer. Then, before long, we were sitting inside the Marina Bay Sands concert hall. The lights dimmed, and the audience hushed in anticipation. The stage came alive, revealing a dynamic set that transported us back in time to the streets of New Jersey. The story unfolded, capturing our hearts with its raw emotion and captivating music.

The actors took the stage, embodying the legendary Four Seasons and bringing their iconic songs to life. From the sweet harmonies of "Sherry" to the soulful ballad of "Can't Take My Eyes Off You," the crowd was immersed in a nostalgic journey through the music that defined an era. With each note and every word, the audience traveled back to a time when music had the power to heal, inspire, and unite. We laughed, cheered, and shed tears of nostalgia as the story of the Four Seasons unfolded before our eyes. By the end of the show, we were on our feet, applauding and singing along with the appreciating crowd.

Leaving the Marina Bay Sands, hand in hand, we couldn't help but feel an overwhelming sense of gratitude for the experience we had just shared. The music was a reminder of the power of art to transport us to another time and place. When the show was over, all I could say was, "Oh, What a Night." It was a memorable night in our life together that we would treasure for eternity.

The following day, when morning broke, I felt tired after a sleepless night reminiscing about last night's stage show. I was looking into Jane's peaceful soul and admiring her beautiful body. Reluctantly, I entangled myself from Jane's body, the desire to linger tempting me to stay. We followed our familiar routine, finding solace in the simplicity of a shared breakfast at Starbucks. With a steaming cup of coffee in hand, we parted ways as Jane ventured off to work, leaving me to navigate the hours alone. Sometimes, in an act of defiance against her boss's unspoken disapproval, I would linger around Jane's workplace, filling the void by stealing moments of affection amidst the monotony. The mere sight of her smile, the stolen touch of her lips from time to time, was enough to melt away the emptiness that consumed the hours.

I counted down the minutes until Jane's shift came to an end. Deep down, I questioned why she continued to toil away, knowing her resignation was imminent. But I dared not voice my doubts, for her contentment and unwavering loyalty spoke volumes. Through it all, Jane remained a beacon of joy, her infectious happiness radiating from every pore. She never complained and never faltered in her commitment to both her work and our relationship. Every kiss she bestowed upon me was filled with an intensity that betrayed her underlying contentment, a silent affirmation of our shared devotion.

Friday night arrived, and with it came a surge of excitement. I had managed to secure two coveted tickets to see Chicago at the illustrious Singapore Esplanade Concert Hall. This legendary band from the seventies held a special place in our hearts, their music ingrained in the fabric of our shared memories. As we entered the concert hall, the anticipation was palpable. The air crackled with electricity, eager whispers floating through the crowd. We took our seats and awaited the moment when the lights would dim and the magic would begin. Then, without warning, the stage erupted in a blaze of light and sound. Chicago appeared before us, their presence commanding and full of life. The years may have etched lines upon their faces, but the fire within still burned bright, transforming them into youthful spirits once more.

From the first strum of the guitar, we were taken back in time. The music reverberated through our souls, echoing the soundtrack of our youth. Each song carried us on a journey of nostalgic dreams, evoking emotions long thought forgotten. With every beat, memories danced in our minds, intertwining with the pulsating rhythm of the music. Their hit songs poured forth like a torrential downpour, washing over us in waves of pure joy. "Hard to Say I'm Sorry" tugged at heartstrings, its lyrics a confession of vulnerability and redemption. "Saturday in the Park" ignited a sense of carefree abandon as we sang along, lost in the infectious melody. And then, in a crescendo of emotions, they unleashed their seminal masterpiece, "If You Leave Me Now," causing tears to well up in our eyes.

Chicago reminded us of the power of music, its ability to transcend time and connect souls. In that concert hall, we hadn't just witnessed a show; we had experienced a tapestry of emotions woven together with the threads of melody and rhythm. And as we walked out into the night, we carried a renewed sense of vitality planted forever in our hearts.

The following Friday night was the band Journey playing at the same venue, and we were there again like loyal groupies. We found ourselves back at the Singapore Esplanade Concert Hall, ready to witness yet another iconic band grace the stage. We were there, eager to immerse ourselves in their timeless music. The aura of the venue was charged with excitement as the lights dimmed, and the crowd roared in anticipation. Journey emerged, radiating an aura of elegance and grace that belied their years. Their new lead singer, a talented Filipino boy, stepped up to the mic, ready to give it his all. As the first notes of "Open Arms" resonate through the hall, emotions surged within us. The music swayed and caressed our souls, filling us with a profound sense of nostalgia. Despite the absence of Steve Perry, the legendary original lead singer, the new vocalist delivered a powerful performance, pouring his heart and soul into the songs.

"Faithfully" carried us on a wave of devotion and longing, its lyrics resonating deep within our hearts. The band played with such enthusiasm; their passion was evident in every chord that echoed through the hall. And when they sang "Don't Stop Believin'," the crowd erupted in unified euphoria, singing along as if their lives depended on it. As the night unfolded, Jane and I found ourselves caught in a whirlwind of euphoria. We danced, we sang, and we surrendered to the magic of the music.

We had one weekend left before leaving Singapore, and this Saturday, I told Jane we would visit Johor Bahru, just across the Malaysian border. Arriving home on Thursday, Jane told me the boss had her passport and refused to give it to her. I had no idea why her boss had her passport, and I had a taste of the boss's attitude already just a few weeks ago. I just said never mind; I will go to work with you tomorrow and ask her to return your passport. I could envision this as a drama, but it would be better if I sorted it out now as we were leaving in a week or so to travel the world.

The following day, as promised, I accompanied Jane to her work and asked her boss politely if she could return Jane's passport. After all, it was hers, and I am sure it is illegal to hold her passport against her will. As predicted, this arrogant woman flatly refused to give the passport back to Jane. I said nothing, but I had a plan that I kept a secret. I left her work and said I would be back in one hour.

I knew already that there would be no point in starting an argument with this arrogant lady.

Instead of this, I visited the local police station and asked for their help, and the policeman seemed surprised at what I told him. He was a very polite man and said he would accompany me to Janes's workplace. On arrival, the boss looked in total shock, and a police officer said to this lady can I talk to you in your office, madam. Five minutes later, the boss lady came out of her office and reluctantly handed Jane her passport. I have no idea what the police officer said to her, but she looked really shaken up after their chat. It was all good news in the end, and the drama with the police could have been avoided with a little common sense.

Early Saturday morning, we were in a taxi to Johor Bahru, and within one hour, we were dropped off at our hotel. The taxi driver was a pure Singaporean and said to be careful because all the criminals live here in this border town. I thought it was an unusual thing to say, and I did not give much credence to his words. The first thing we did was get a whole-body Swedish massage at our hotel before wandering around this growing Gem city sitting on the southern tip of Malaysia. By Sunday night, we were back in Singapore with just one week remaining before our planned escape.

Three days from leaving Singapore, it was back to Marina Bay Sands for the stage show called "Rock of Ages," which is a jukebox musical built around the classic rock songs of the 80s. The first chords rang out, and we were instantly transported to a world of neon lights, big hair, and electrifying energy that permeated the air. From the anthems of Bon Jovi to the rebellious spirit of Poison, every song was brought to life with stunning performances that drew us deeper into the storyline.

The actors were performing in perfect harmony on stage, their voices filled with raw emotion. We couldn't help but be swept away by their talent. The story began, combining the songs seamlessly, each number becoming a stepping stone on the Journey of these characters' lives. We sang along, surrendering ourselves entirely to the infectious energy of the performance.

Time seemed to distort, stretching and compressing as the show unfolded. The music became our lifeline, carrying us through a whirlwind of sentiments and memories. As the final notes of the last song echoed through the theater, we rose to our feet, joining the thunderous applause and cheers of the audience. The cast took their bows, basking in the well-deserved adulation for their stellar performances.

Leaving the theater that night, the magic of "Rock of Ages" had fused with the electrifying spirit of the city, leaving an indelible mark on our souls. As we held hands walking into the night, I couldn't help but smile, knowing that these moments would forever be cherished, stored in the depths of our hearts. After a fantastic month in Singapore, it was time for Jane to leave her work, and even with the anxious protests by her boss, we bid her and this country bye-bye for now. Singapore was home to Jane for almost six years, but now it was her time to explore the world and what it offered to me.

We were heading to Changi Airport for a trip to Thailand for one month to see what we could see and to do whatever flowed in our path. The song playing on the radio was an old 70s song that I told Jane to listen to carefully. "I never promised you a rose garden; along with the sunshine, there's gonna be a little rain sometimes." Jane smiled and understood precisely the song's meaning, and no further words were needed, only her smile that said it all. Our life's Journey was now beginning, and where it would take us, only the universe could know that answer.

Chapter 4

Bangkok and Pattaya Thailand.

Upon check-in at the Cathay Pacific desk, the lady from the counter said we had been upgraded to business class. It seemed the universe was aligned, and when this happens, we must keep the alignment intact and not fluctuate. Before long, we were sitting in a comfortable chair with a glass of French champagne. "Cheers, darling!" was all I needed to say as we were waiting for the takeoff. As we drank our last sip, the waitress warmly smiled as she took our empty glasses. The bubbles played tricks with my feelings as I squeezed Jane's hand tight.

Then, before I had time to think, the Airbus 330 was speeding down the runway and rocketed into the sky with the reassuring sound of the landing gear folding back in position beneath us, and we were on our way to Thailand, the city of temples. I was holding my darling's hand, and we both were smiling with sheer contentment and excitement that can only be felt when you know you are with your destiny and totally in love. This was the beginning of our travels that would take us to places we only ever dreamed of visiting.

It was a short two-hour flight with the friendly flight attendants serving mouthwatering food and keeping our champagne glasses topped up. The aircraft descended gracefully, touching down in Bangkok, the bustling capital city. The upgrade to the business class set the tone for our entire trip to Thailand. It reminded us to take the unexpected, savor every moment, and never lose sight of the magic that can unfold when we least expect it.

I could have stayed on this plane forever, but now we had landed and were lined up at the Immigration. Thanks to the wonderful upgrade to business class, which gave us the privilege of going through the fast lane, which expedited our arrival. After completing this job, we looked at our passports, and our reward was a stamp that said we could stay in the Kingdom of Thailand for thirty days. The journey from the airport to our hotel was a sensory overload – vibrant colors, exotic scents, and the symphony of street sounds engulfed us. Thailand's charm and allure were palpable, containing us in a sense of wonder and curiosity.

With shackles broken and barriers shattered, we held the ethereal energy of Bangkok, knowing that the next chapter of our lives was ready to be written. The past would remain just that – a distant memory, fading away like whispers in the wind. Arriving by way of a yellow-colored taxi, we soon were at the JW Marriott hotel in the Sukhumvit area. This was a tourist area, maybe only second to the notorious Patpong. Now, it was time to unwind and start living the dream after the past month of being bound by shackles from the work of Jane.

We were not merely commencing a vacation but stepping into a chapter of our lives where dreams transformed into reality. With six months of exploration and discovery stretched before us, we were primed to unravel the mysteries of each destination. Singapore served as our departure point, a tantalizing appetizer before the main course of our global escapades.

Thailand promised a tapestry of luminous landscapes, rich cultural heritage, and spiritual enlightenment. The allure of ancient temples beckoned us, whispering tales of wisdom and spirituality that had stood the test of time. We hungered for the knowledge and serenity that these hallowed grounds offered.

We swiftly threw our bags into the room, which had the scent of lemongrass teasing our senses. We were already primed to let our hair down, thanks to the French champagne onboard our flight. We found a band playing nearby our hotel dressed like the Beatles right down to the mop hairstyles and only played Beatles songs, which gave a nostalgic feel. My memory rewound to the early sixties, and I imagined we were in the popular Cavern Club in Liverpool, England. My mind was now free to imagine and explore like the past was present, and even the future was past. What that means is nothing mattered that was deeper than a shallow stream. In my life, I noticed that thinking and analyzing life too much took away the present moment that was to be lived.

Yesterday was gone, and tomorrow would still be there, and so is now. We were instantly on the dance floor, and Jane was now dancing with a young Thai girl while I moved to the music solo. Jane and her newfound friend looked good together and were both natural in their sharp dance moves. I was hallucinating momentarily and imagined it was Ginger Rogers and Rita Haywood moving to the beat of "The Fab Four." Jane did confide in me that she sometimes had girlfriends. She informed me that next week, we were to meet her old girlfriend from Singapore. Her friend's name was Yuli, and she was now staying in Pattaya, about two hours from Bangkok.

Back at the present moment, the two girls were looking sweet at the bar as we shared a beer. Rapidly, time moved, and before we knew it, the time was now 1 a.m., and the bar was closing. The saying "time flies when you're having fun" was a gross understatement. Hours seemed like minutes, and I could not fathom where the past four hours went. We then reluctantly bid farewell to our newfound friend after a sensual wet kiss on the lips. She kissed Jane and me as well, which gave a feeling of excitement to us both. The wave of excitement coursed through us, igniting a flame of exhilaration that danced in our veins. Our journey home was filled with tender kisses, each one sealing the memories of a day well-lived, a day filled with thrilling encounters and newfound connections.

As we finally drifted off to sleep, exhaustion mingled with the intoxicating thrill of the day. The world seemed to stand still, allowing us to revel in the boundless joy that can only be found in letting go and fully embracing the present moment. Yesterday was a memory, and tomorrow held promises yet to be fulfilled. At that moment, now was all that mattered.

As the sun rose, we planned to check out the sites around this wonderful, exhilarating, effervescent city. We explored the Grand Palace in its entire splendor in the heart of town. The Palace was a group of yellow and gold dazzling temples. Here, they claimed this was the home of the King of Siam since 1782.

Then, by early evening, we had made our way to the well-known Patpong markets where, every day, the traffic would be halted, and makeshift markets were constructed. They sold anything from top-named handbags to designer shirts, but of course, all were perfect copies of the original product. Imagine three hundred and sixty-five days a year; they would construct these markets at 6 p.m., and then at

2 a.m., they would pull it all down, ready for traffic to use the next day.

Our journey continued as we made our way to Khao San Road, a unique street that beckoned travelers from all corners of the globe. This bustling haven was renowned as the ultimate destination for backpackers seeking new places, camaraderie, and a taste of the wild nightlife. The street came alive with contagious energy. Music thumped from every corner, inviting passersby to join in the revelry. The air was filled with laughter, the clinking of glasses, and the sweet scent of freedom. Backpackers from all walks of life mingled effortlessly, sharing stories of their journeys and bonding over their shared love for exploration.

We couldn't resist the allure of this spirited street and decided to immerse ourselves in the stimulating atmosphere. We danced and laughed with newfound friends, connecting with people from every corner of the world. It was a melting pot of cultures, a testament to the beauty of human connection and the common desire to seek new experiences. As the night wore on, we reluctantly tore ourselves away from the festivities, knowing that tomorrow would bring a full-day tour of the infamous River Kwai. In anticipation of our day ahead, we bid our fellow revelers goodnight and retired to our quarters.

The tour took us through the bustling streets of Bangkok, passing by crowded markets and towering skyscrapers. Soon, we arrived at the River Kwai, a place of historical significance and natural beauty. As we stepped off the bus, we were greeted by a local guide who led us to the legendary bridge over the River Kwai. The bridge stood as a testament to the thousands of prisoners of war who had suffered and died during its construction in World War II. The atmosphere was solemn, yet the surrounding lush greenery added a touch of tranquility.

We walked along the bridge, feeling the weight of the past beneath our feet. The river flowed gently below, its calm waters reflecting the golden sun. It was a hauntingly beautiful sight, reminding us of the sacrifices made by those who came before us. We arrived home as darkness fell over the temple city and slept well as we were very content but tired from our full day of travels.

As the morning sun painted the sky with colors of orange and pink, we set out on a new escapade, this time to the entertainment city of Pattaya, known by some as "Sin City." It was a place that carried a reputation for wild nights and untamed desires. Our journey took us down the winding roads, stretching for miles as anticipation mingled with curiosity in the air. Jane's Singaporean friend Yuli, would be meeting us tonight in Walking Street for dinner. My expectations were not high, but if I knew what would transpire after our meeting, I would have been totally on another planet, so maybe it was a good thing that I was cool and calm.

It was a warm afternoon, and there was no better place to be than the hotel swimming pool, surrounded by palm trees nestled amongst perfectly landscaped gardens and statues of Thai Gods. They were all here by the pool, namely Indra, Ganesh, Brahma, and Hanuman, to name four. This tranquil area was perfect, with the cool blue water soothing my eyes and refreshing my mind. After a relaxing afternoon by the pool, it was soon twilight time, a signal to get ready for the meeting with Yuli.

The Walking Street was called for the reason that each night it was closed to traffic and was only for feet and no vehicles and full of entertainment and the number one red-light district of Pattaya. It was just a short stroll from our hotel, and we trekked along the waterfront. Here, there were many ladies of all ages, shapes, and sizes, and even men dressed as a woman for those who needed or felt the urge to walk on the "wild side of life." Pattaya certainly lived up to the name of Sin City with dancing girl bars, discos, and many drinking bars.

Jane and I chose a drinking bar with a band starting later, and Jane texted Yuli where we were to meet. We ordered a couple of ice-cold Singha beers, the local Thai beer. It was almost 7 p.m., the time to meet up with Yuli. Jane was dressed very alluring that night then from a distance, I noticed a young lady walking towards our bar wrapped in a short red dress and long brown hair flowing down the back of the dress, almost reaching as far as her sexy bottom.

Before I knew it, this girl and Jane were hugging tight and kissing with wet kisses on each other's lips. I was surprised when she introduced herself as she then gave me a sweet kiss and a gentle hug. She was happy to see Jane, and it seemed they were more than friends in Singapore, which I was glad to know. Jane was honest and said she likes girls. We all drank, danced, and laughed, drinking ice-cold Singha beers, and people noticed me with two gorgeous girls, and it seemed I was the luckiest man in Pattaya. The band played loud and hard, and we partied hard, also. I think, at times, I was dreaming and had a vision. I was on another planet deep in space in the vicinity of the Milky Way.

It was almost midnight, and now we were all being affectionate like it did not matter and not discreet in the slightest. We had enough to drink, and we strolled back to the hotel, wrapped in a cloud of laughter and intoxication, and the night took on an air of mystery and anticipation. The moonlight danced upon our faces, casting gentle shadows that painted a picture of enchantment.

Arriving at the hotel, our steps quickened with excitement as if propelled by an invisible force. The whispers of desire echoed in the corridors as we found ourselves standing before the door of our room, the threshold to a world of possibilities. Inside, the air crackled with electricity, charged with the raw energy of newfound connections. The room became a canvas upon which our passions collided and merged to create a masterpiece of unspoken desires. Amid swirling emotions, our bodies became vessels for the language of love. Time seemed to stand still as our souls combined, blending into one harmonious symphony of pleasure and connection.

There existed a unique bond between three individuals - Yuli, Jane, and myself. Yuli's hunger for connection was evident. Her lips met mine with an intensity that sent excitement through my body. Surrounded by the steam and the whispers of soft moans, Jane's presence became a testament to her open-mindedness and willingness to share her love.

With each touch and caress, we shed our desires that flowed freely. A deep sense of pleasure resonated throughout the room. Passion took hold as we moved from the shower to the bed, where the exploration intensified. Jane and Yuli reveled in each other's taste, their bodies bound with pleasure. And then, with an insatiable hunger, I gave myself wholly to Yuli, plunging deep into her wetness.

The hours that followed transcended mere words. It was a symphony of sensuality, a crescendo of ecstasy that defied any attempt at description. Our connection was primal, untamed, a union of bodies and souls lost in the euphoria of each other's touch. In that moment, we were bound by the intoxicating power of pleasure. As the night drew to a close, we found ourselves tangled in a web of limbs, drifting into a tranquil slumber. The air around us was infused with the scent of our passionate encounters, a reminder of the uninhibited love we had shared.

Morning broke, casting a gentle glow upon our tangled bodies in the room. The night had unfolded like pages from a forbidden book, filled with secrets shared only by moonlight and whispered promises. But as daylight was upon us, a bittersweet realization settled into the room – our paths diverged, destined to walk separate journeys. Our world is filled with endless possibilities. Jane and I extended an invitation to Yuli to join us and be our companion together on a journey to the enchanting destination of Phuket, which she accepted, brimming with anticipation for the experiences that awaited us.

For the next week, we were all inseparable, and I am sure people were envious of what was happening. It was a dream that was reality, or as they say, I was living the dream and reflecting the beauty of the moments we would share. Phuket would become more than just a destination; it would become a chapter in our continuing story together.

Chapter 5

Phuket Thailand

Time moved along, and the Earth rotated, now I was on a Thai Airlines plane for a one-hour flight south to Phuket with two beautiful women by my side. Known for its open-minded, party atmosphere, I had a feeling the three of us would fit well into this city. For the next two weeks, I was expecting excitement and fun as we all discreetly sat relaxed and cool on our flight that was as "smooth as silk." After a smooth landing, we gathered our bags and were soon in a taxi for our forty-minute ride to Patong Beach.

I checked into our hotel without any worries, and the lady at the front desk could not control her smile as she knew what was happening as I would have two girls with me, and only one bed in our room. As we entered our room, it looked perfect with a huge king-sized bed and large bathtub and even a bowl of fresh fruit waiting to be eaten nestled in a decorative colorful bowl covered with pictures of elephants. Not even a few minutes went past before our clothes were stripped from our eager bodies and thrown wherever they landed, and we made fantasy love before sleeping deep and awakening early.

I walked into breakfast, and people glanced at us, but no one cared, and we, indeed, did not care. Happiness was beaming brightly from our faces, and this was as good as life could get. I was like an ancient King with two heavenly queens beside him, and the Gods were smiling down on me and whispering soft words like relish and adore my gifts. As we indulged in a delicious breakfast, our joy was palpable. The warmth of the sun caressed our skin, and the sweet scent of tropical fruits filled the air. It felt like the universe conspired to create this perfect moment, granting us a taste of paradise. With every sip of freshly squeezed orange juice, we reveled in the simple pleasures of life. The laughter in the distance intertwined with the gentle lapping of waves on the nearby shore, creating a symphony that echoed our blissful state.

After savoring a great meal that was delicious and nutritious in every sense of the word, we walked around for a while, searching out the boutiques for a swimsuit each. We found a shop that sold us matching tan colored and yellow flowered swimmers. The two girls, or wives as it would be for the next two weeks, had a one-piece swimsuit and me a tight boxer-type swim shorts, and the good thing was, we all matched, and all looked like we were a treble.

We walked down to beautiful Patong Beach, only a five-minute walk from our hotel, and we were soon in the blue crystal water cooling off when my mind went back to when a Tsunami struck at this very spot-on boxing day in 2004, killing many tourists and locals and devastating the inhabitants of this popular tourist beach.

As I frolicked in the gentle waves, the weight of the past tragedy hung heavy in the air. It was impossible to ignore the haunting remnants of the past, the echoes of a disaster that had forever changed the lives of those who called Patong Beach home. In the distance, the serene horizon seemed to stretch endlessly, its beauty belying the horrors it had witnessed. The waves whispered their secrets, carrying tales of resilience and survival. And amidst the joyous laughter and playful splashing, a sense of reverence settled upon me.

I looked at my girls, my eyes reflecting an understanding. I knew that this moment, this exhilarating swim in the same waters where so many lives were lost, held a more profound significance. It was a testament to the indomitable human spirit, a celebration of life and healing power. The three of us bobbed in the azure sea; we played and laughed and were like we owned this beach, and no one or nothing existed except us three on this beach with fine, clean yellow sand and warm, inviting waters.

Back at the hotel, we filled the huge bathtub with warm water and emptied many bath bubbles before we all climbed into the bath, which was built for three, maybe two, but we were not big people, so we fitted well. Slowly washing all the sand from our bodies, we all dressed simply for a night out. The girls looked sexy and unusual, wearing colorful, short-flowered dresses. We then made our way uptown as nightlife was the real existence for young people. I was feeling twenty-one years of age, and my wife looked eighteen.

In the heart of the pulsating city, we surrendered ourselves to the wild nightlife that beckoned us. The streets buzzed with energy, each corner offering a new experience waiting to be discovered. And as we strolled through the neon-lit lanes, smiles and anticipation painted our faces.

Entering a dimly lit bar filled with the melodies of a live band, we found ourselves amidst a kaleidoscope of emotions. The music wrapped around us, embracing our souls and inviting our bodies to sway to its rhythm. We joined the dancing crowd, surrendering to the euphoria that surged through our veins. The Russian bar, with its exotic ambiance, seemed like a world of its own. The staff greeted us with warm smiles, and the enchanting dancers captivated our attention with their graceful movements. They spun and twirled their colorful costumes, adding to the allure of the night.

Around us, the crowd pulsed with joy, their laughter mingling with the beat of the music. Time seemed to stand still as we danced the night away, our bodies moving in perfect harmony with the intoxicating melodies. With each step, we shed the weight of the mundane, embracing the freedom that only exists in such moments. As the night wore on, we found ourselves swaying to retro tunes that stirred nostalgia within us. The lyrics were etched in our hearts, transporting us to a time long gone. And as we sang along, our voices intermingled with those around us, creating a symphony of collective memories.

We all loved this time in exciting Patong Beach, where our residence or hotel served each day a complimentary breakfast that we savored, and after breakfast, we would endure a long run on its yellow sands and swim in the clear blue water. Tomorrow, we had organized a speed boat trip to tour around the islands, so we had an early night in preparation for our trip starting at 7 a.m.

All three of us woke early with the sun beaming through the half-closed curtains, telling me to awaken and get ready as I inhaled the sweet smell of sex that filled the room from the night before, and it was a perfume to my senses. We were waiting in the foyer for our day's island hopping, and it was not long before a smiling Thai van driver greeted us warmly and guided us to his modern, white-looking van. Then he shuttled us to our boat, parked on the water with about eight others of European descent onboard our transportation.

The other passengers were all glancing with curiosity at the luckiest man in the world with his two young sweethearts. Sometimes, I paused and imagined I was dreaming the most vivid dream imaginable, but in truth, it was reality. I was like an ancient prince or even a noble king, pushing each day to the limits of fun-filled happiness. My humble gratitude couldn't help but thank the Gods who blessed me with the riches of love and happiness. The boat gently rocked on the water, enticing us to board.

The boat's motor then woke me from my dazed state, and all passengers cheered as the speed boat rocketed off from the shore and sped away to our first destination towards the morning sun across calm still waters. Phi Phi, Krabi, and James Bond Island, to name a few, stops on our day ahead. We snorkeled with our matching swimmers and talked and drank cold beers with our curious European co-passengers. We had fun all day, and people and their eyes watched me kiss, hug, and show sweetness to my girls all day, and I noticed I inspired the other couples to be sweet to each other.

With each passing moment, the cool breeze carried whispers of excitement, mingling with laughter and the excited chatter of fellow travelers. As we sailed between islands, the world seemed to transform into a striking collage of colors, with crystal-clear waters glistening in shades of turquoise and emerald. Every island held its unique charm, offering hidden coves, picturesque beaches, and lush landscapes waiting to be explored. Together, we adopted each destination, immersing ourselves in the natural wonders that surrounded us. From snorkeling amidst coral reefs teeming with life to hiking winding trails through tropical jungles, we savored every moment as if it were a gift from the heavens.

As the day drew to a close, memories carved themselves deeply within our hearts. I realized that we were living not just a dream but a reality- one that seemed too surreal and beautiful to be true. We celebrated our journey, our hearts filled with gratitude and our spirits soaring. We had discovered that happiness wasn't simply a destination but a path; we walked together, every step a testament to our unwavering love for one another.

At sunset, we were home a little tired and sunburned, but we had a quick shower to freshen up, and we were ready for a party night with our bodies running on pure adrenalin. We did not need to rest, and after a short ten-minute stroll, we arrived back at the Russian bar that we hung out at the first night we went out. We were a little primed already after a few beers on our island-hopping tour. We sat and toasted each other with an ice-cold Singha beer, touching our dry, eager lips.

Before we had time to talk, a tall blonde Russian lady about forty years of age entered the bar with movie star looks and dressed like a lady who was no ordinary woman and smiled curiously at the two girls who were looking sweet and were kissing. As for me, I was sitting quietly on the opposite side of the table. The girls were stunned by this lady's beauty, more so by how she presented herself as she was not young but very gorgeous to the point of suggesting she was stunning.

She looked a little sad and lonely, so I cautiously and respectfully said, "Please join us." She did hesitate but then sat beside me, and her sad smile changed to one of happiness, and I said, "Can I buy you a beer?". She said yes, and we all clunked our beers together and cheered. The beautiful lady admitted she was not a big drinker and had not had a beer in years as she only drank wine and champagne, so this was an excellent icebreaker.

As the night progressed, the once-guarded expression on her face gave way to a relaxed demeanor. The softness of her voice mingled with the laughter and music around us, enveloping us in an atmosphere of serene joy. The girls, now intoxicated by the freedom of the night, took to the dance floor, their movements a graceful expression of liberation. We asked her no questions except her name, to which she replied, "My name is Veronica." I doubt it was her real name, judging by how she hesitated with her answer, but who cares? This name gave a sense that she was from an ancient Greek or Latin time. Her voice was soft and alluring, and after her second beer, her body language seemed more relaxed, and she smiled contentedly.

The girls were now dancing, leaving me alone with Veronica, and I chatted a shallow talk with no questions needed. Veronica, as she called herself, remained an enigma throughout the evening. She carried a mystical quality, as if she belonged to a character from a forgotten era. We refrained from prying into her past, content with her company without unearthing the secrets she held within. After all, I had no right to question this lady. I ordered three Mojito cocktails as I just drank another ice-cold beer. The girls began to be a little tipsy, and soon, the three girls were dancing to slow songs on the empty dance floor, but prying eyes were glued to this event, especially mine.

Arriving back at the table, three more cocktails awaited the lips of three beauties to savor. Not a soul could divert their gaze from the sight unfolding before them. The three beauties, uninhibited by judgment, swayed to the rhythm of the music, lost in an intoxicating dance. It was in that moment, amidst the pulsating energy of the bar, that I found myself holding Veronica's hand, drawn to her in a way beyond explanation. Our eyes locked, and without hesitation, she pressed her lips to me.

In that stolen kiss, the taste of strawberries, sweet and irresistible, mingled with the rush of adrenaline coursing through my veins. Oblivious to the world around us, the girls, too consumed by their desires, were lost in their passionate exchange. For no reason at all, it felt natural to hold the hand of this Russian blonde beauty. Then, looking into her eyes, I pressed my lips to hers and gave another wet kiss that tasted again like the sweetest strawberry I could imagine possible. The girls were not even watching. They were already intoxicated and were also kissing on the dance floor. I loved the way these two girls just took pleasure in the moment without caring about the thoughts of others who were noticing them.

The noise of the bar, overwhelming and invasive, urged me to seek solace in a more intimate setting. With a silent invitation, Veronica agreed to accompany us to our hotel bar, unburdened by hesitation or doubt. Hand in hand, we left the pulsating chaos behind, stepping into a realm where time stood still. The hotel bar, now bathed in subdued lighting, whispered of unspoken possibilities. And in that moment, as the night led us into its tender embrace, we surrendered to the unpredictability of fate. Veronica, with her mysterious allure, had defied expectations, and together, we delved into a world where inhibitions were shattered and the boundaries of connection blurred.

We found a lovely table outside the hotel bar, where I ordered a bottle of Moet champagne, and four glasses were poured by the young bar attendant. As we settled into a quiet corner, each sip of our drinks mingled with the weight of anticipation. He smiled jealously but approvingly to me as we watched the bubbles bouncing from side to side of the glasses. We were unaware of all the people where we sat and sipped this sweet French drink. I kissed Veronica again, and she was excited by the kisses and asked the girls if it was okay.

Jane and Yuli, who were not jealous in the slightest, said, "Relax and just have a good time with our husband." Before long, Veronica was sitting on my lap and being touched discreetly. She was excited and could not hold back the build-up of wetness in her thighs. After finishing our drink, we were soon in the room, and the girls were both kissing this gorgeous lady who had movie star looks. I tasted her wetness eagerly and made love to Veronica while she was being kissed passionately by the girls. Behind closed doors, hidden from prying eyes, our encounter continued a dance of souls intertwined in a symphony of raw desire. Four souls found themselves entangled in a night of unforgettable passion. It was as if the universe had conspired to bring us together, if only for a fleeting moment.

Veronica, a mysterious and enchanting lady, had graced us with her presence. With her movie star looks and a hint of sadness in her eyes, she captured the hearts of all who laid their gaze upon her. Inhibitions faded away, replaced by an electric energy that pulsed through the room. Underneath the twinkling stars, we all found solace in the secrecy of the night. Kisses were like fireworks, igniting a flame that burned brightly. Veronica, not bound by conventional norms, followed the desires of her heart, finding pleasure in the touch of each lover.

4 a.m. arrived after a few hours of sleep, and Veronica said, "Sorry, I have to leave now." She kissed us all and said thank you for a wonderful night, and she confessed maybe it was the best night of her life. No phone numbers or emails were exchanged, and we all were left with a remembrance inside our memory bank. We never saw Veronica again. It was like she appeared from heaven, given just a one-night leave pass, and then returned, and maybe she was at this time being scolded by the Gods

when she arrived back in heaven. We all knew she had a big secret, but none of us cared, as this would be a memory we would hold in our minds forever.

We just continued our lives and enjoyed our beach days, dancing and partying, and, of course, my fantasy nights, sharing two young, sexy, happy sweethearts. This is how it was. Life moves, changes happen, and all things must end, at least for this time in my life. Yuli, with her infectious smile and vivacious spirit, had entered our lives like a whirlwind. Together, we painted the canvas of our days with fun and youthful exuberance. Beach days were spent basking under the golden rays as the waves caressed our toes, carrying away our worries on every receding tide.

Amid dance floors and pulsating beats, we surrendered to the music and let our bodies weave a story of passion and liberation. With each twirl and sway, we found contentment in the rhythm of our hearts, creating cherished memories while leaving footprints in the sand.

As the final days drew near, a bittersweet sentiment filled the air. The realization that Yuli's time in this place was coming to an end couldn't dampen the magic that had been shared. It was not sadness that prevailed but rather a deep sense of contentment for the beautiful moments we had woven together.

With tearful goodbyes, we hugged one last time, sealing the bond with promises of reunion. With whispers and tender kisses, we vowed to meet again in the enchanting Lion City of Singapore one year from that very moment. Jane and I had a different path to travel and were ready to explore the world and see what this big, wonderful, exciting, ever-changing world had to offer us. We were free, and our attitude toward life was open-minded.

Chapter 6

Hong Kong.

In the chambers of my heart, a treasured memory existed that had brought us closer than ever before. In a display of trust and devotion, Jane had introduced her gorgeous and vivacious friend into our exciting life, igniting a passion that burned like an eternal flame. It was in those moments that I knew without a doubt that Jane was the woman I wished to share my life with. Her uniqueness and her precious attitude were a treasure beyond compare.

I was now alone with my destiny princess Jane, and love was floating in the air. Today, we would travel to Hong Kong, branded as Asia's world city, for only four days and then onto Shenzhen, Taiwan, and then we would explore Japan. Afterward, we will head to Las Vegas, where I secretly planned to marry my gorgeous, sweet Jane. Love was weaving through my every breath as we began our take off on a journey that would shape our lives forever.

I had been to Hong Kong many times in my past life before finding my destiny, but this was the first time for Jane. This was an exciting city with skyscrapers surrounding its picturesque harbor where in days gone by, Junks and San Pans sailed the harbor waters with many families living simple but contented on their boat homes. Today, these were distant memories gone except for a few boats remaining for the amusement of tourists.

We stayed at the majestic Renaissance Hotel, looking over the harbor in Wanchai. At night, I guided Jane to the main area of Lockhart Road, where we spent our first night listening to a talented Filipino band playing at one of the numerous drinking bars in this area. The music was first-class, and the appreciative crowd was amazed at the quality of the lead singer's voice. This girl had a gift, and perhaps someday, her songbird voice would be discovered. The universe had a way of weaving dreams into reality.

Our next journey had now begun in the bustling city, renowned as the Jewel in the Orient. With four days of exploration, we plunged ourselves into the culture and exquisite cuisine. We wandered through bustling streets, gazing at towering skyscrapers that seemed to caress the heavens. Together, we shared conversations with locals, for every moment spent together was a way of new learnings.

On a chilly morning, Jane and I wanted to visit the newly opened wonderous theme park Disneyland. Rugged up in our warm jackets, we boarded the train that would take us to this magical realm of joy and wonder. The two lovers were riding the train to the popular amusement park after we had ridden the iconic double-deck tram in this city that made everything accessible to all travelers to explore.

As we set foot in Disneyland, the happy atmosphere infused our spirits with childlike glee. Laughter filled the air as we eagerly explored every corner, indulging in the thrilling rides and captivating shows. It was as if time had receded, and we became big kids once again, reveling in the joy that only a place like this could bring. We were having fun and enjoying all the attractions in the park. The rides and shows were exciting, and we even shook hands with our favorite character, Mickey Mouse.

As the day waned, Jane and I boarded the old-fashioned tram that ascended with determination up the steep mountain. The slow ascent only heightened our anticipation, with a breathtaking view that awaited us. At last, we reached the summit after just climbing to 396 meters above sea level. Reaching the peak, looking over the city lights that gave us a feeling we were sitting right at the very top of the world. We settled into Bubba Gumps Restaurant, our eyes feasting not only on the delectable fresh shrimp but also on the panoramic city lights that danced below us. The sight was awe-inspiring, a testament to the beauty and grandeur that Hong Kong offered.

The sun rose on a new day, and our next experience awaited us at Ocean Park. More memories after another beautiful, fun-filled day were stored inside our hearts. As the night was upon us, we journeyed to Happy Valley Racecourse, steeped in the racing calendar. The sight of thoroughbreds galloping under the mesmerizing glow of lights stirred the adrenaline in our veins. The atmosphere was electric, crackling with anticipation as the locals cheered and shouted, their voices merging into a harmonious uproar.

Here, I caught up with my old Jockey friend Neil, who was denied his license to ride in Hong Kong because of his association with people with "Triad" connections. Neil was now a hardened drinker and made his living from advising illegal bookmakers what he knew, and with a little inside information, he lived well. I asked no questions and made no judgment, and we just reminisced about his riding days when Neil was a fearless rider and even remembered some of the victory rides on the horses that I owned at the time.

Here at Happy Valley Racecourse, the thoroughbreds raced under lights every Wednesday night in the racing season, which is from September to late June. The loud shouting and cheering from the locals as the horses rounded the last turn into the straight was deafening. Here, some won their fortunes, and others lost their fortunes, but they would still return the following Wednesday night to try and lose their winnings or recover their losses from the week before.

Tonight was exceptional as Jane experienced the exhilaration of horse racing for the first time. Her eyes widened with wonder as the thundering hooves echoed through her being, and the crowd's passion excited her senses. That night, she understood the allure and the magic that drew people to this intoxicating sport. Outside the racetrack, we caught up again with Neil, and he looked nervous, looking around with fear on his face. I sensed something was not as it should be, and his body language was a total turnaround from earlier in the night. His cheerful smiling face had turned to terror, likened to someone facing the hangman's noose.

Then, suddenly, from the darkened shadows, three hefty Chinese men came out of nowhere and started talking to Neil. We were ordered to keep walking, and there was no argument from me as these guys looked like they would cut your throat instantly if you did not follow their command. As I looked back, the three men punched Neil to the ground and then kicked him for several minutes on the ground. They then left the scene in a black van that pulled up and sped away.

With a heavy heart, I rushed back to the scene where the tragedy unfolded before my eyes. Neil, once a resilient jockey, now lay motionless on the unforgiving concrete sidewalk. Blood stained his mouth, and an eerie stillness had replaced the fear that had gripped him moments ago.

I knelt beside my fallen friend, desperately hoping for signs of life. With trembling hands, I gently touched Neil's neck, my heart sinking as I felt the coldness of his skin on my fingertips. It felt like time stood still, the world holding its breath in collective disbelief. Summoning every ounce of courage within me, I steadfastly refused to accept defeat. I called out for help, waving down a passerby, my voice filled with desperation and urgency. Minutes felt like an eternity as I waited, hoping my friend would survive this terrifying ordeal.

Soon, a police car was on the scene, and then an ambulance and Neil was loaded carefully inside, and then a deafening siren whaled, and the lights flashed. I could not help my friend now, and it seemed he was in good hands. And I only hoped he was still alive. The best thing to do now was to get myself and Jane out of this area and return by taxi to the safety of the hotel. I did not want these people to assume that whatever Neil did or was involved in deserved this fate that we were involved. Before Neil was whisked away, I grasped his hand, my voice filled with unspoken emotions. "Hold on, my old friend," I whispered my words, a silent plea for his strength.

Morning broke, bringing with it a renewed sense of purpose. I knew I had to gather more information to understand what had befallen my old friend. With determination on my face, I made my way to the main hospital, leaving Jane at the hotel for her safety.

In the bustling corridors of the hospital, I felt a mix of anxiety and anticipation as I approached the reception desk. I explained my connection to Neil and inquired about his whereabouts and condition. The receptionist, with a kind smile, directed me to the ward where Neil was being treated. As I stepped into the room, I was met with an array of medical equipment and the hushed whispers of nurses and doctors attending to various patients. There lying in a sterile hospital bed was Neil, still frail but unmistakably alive. I felt nervous and worried as I approached my dear friend, grasping his hand gently. A wave of relief washed over me, knowing that Neil had overcome the worst of his ordeal.

On our last day in Hong Kong, we put the previous night out of our minds, knowing the good news that my friend survived his ordeal, even though his jaw was broken, and also was nursing several cracked ribs and other broken bones. Neil would leave Hong Kong as soon as he was well enough to fly, which might be a few weeks considering his injuries.

We visited the crowded markets of the city, ending up at the Stanley Street markets. It was a somber day, but I always tried to keep a face that showed Jane all was good and no problems. I learned a lot from last night and realized if I followed the fork in the road that Neil chose, I could have suffered the same fate. I only hoped he would learn from this fast life pattern he chose that ended in peril. He also would embark on a new road in life's highway. As the day drew to a close, Jane and I basked in the warmth of the hotel's heated swimming pool, and our bodies relaxed against the water's soothing embrace. The city's grandeur seemed to melt away at that moment, leaving only the two of us and a sense of tranquility amidst the bustling metropolis.

Refreshed and rejuvenated, we ventured out into the busy streets once more, making our way to Kowloon to witness the spectacle that awaited us. The symphony of lights across Victoria Harbour danced and shimmered, painting the evening sky with a kaleidoscope of colors. Each burst of light held a story of its own, capturing the attention and imagination of all who gazed upon it. The Star Ferry, a timeless vessel that connected the bustling districts of Wanchai and Kowloon, carried us across the harbor, providing us with a front-row seat to the enchanting spectacle. As we stood on the ferry's deck, the cool breeze kissed our faces, heightening our senses and amplifying the magic of the moment.

Our time in Hong Kong had been brief but filled with unforgettable experiences. Our minds shifted to Shenzhen as we were now in a taxi for our noon departure to Shekou, a sixty-minute ferry trip across the calm waters of the Pearl River Delta.

Chapter 7

Shenzhen and Taiwan.

We had a booking at the Nanhai Hotel, where my good friend Steve was the resident singer. My friend was now living the dream with a harem of young girls from Hong Kong to Shenzhen that kept him occupied.

Steve possessed a gift, a talent honed by years of dedication to his craft. With his nimble fingers caressing the strings of his acoustic guitar and his soulful voice captivating hearts, he had the power to move even the most ignorant in the crowd. The potential for stardom had always lingered within his grasp, yet he chose a different path, content with the life he had created at the Nanhai.

Steve greeted Jane and me at the Ferry Terminal with warm hugs and a firm handshake, and he had a grin from ear to ear. I think he was a little surprised that I was engaged and soon to be married, as my past life resembled the road Steve was now following. We had a plan tonight to visit the Polo Club owned by his close friend Phillip, who had lived a colorful past life, but for now, he ran a club and restaurant known throughout the city as the place to go. Phillip had reinvented himself, transforming from a man of entangled pasts into an excellent, relaxed club owner.

Arriving at the Polo Club and meeting Phillip gave me a good feeling as this man was a welcoming person with a warm heart. He greeted Jane and me with open arms and a magnetic charm that drew everyone to him. His stories flickered in his eyes, mingling with the laughter that echoed throughout the space. In the presence of this remarkable man, I couldn't help but be reminded that life is a journey woven with countless threads of experience, each one contributing to the masterpiece we become.

As the night unfolded, the stage came alive with a group of talented Filipino musicians. Their melodies come from all eras of time, from the rock and roll of the 60s to the anthems of the 80s. I felt happiness drifting through the air. Phillip joined Steve and me at our table, and we all talked about events that were but a flash of our past. I think the three of us had different pasts, but really, some similarities were distinctive. Phillip treated his staff with kindness and care, and the attitude of his workers showed that they had the ultimate respect for their Boss. As it was now 1 a.m., we bid farewell to our friends and to a club that was second to none in this seaside town.

Waking late the following day, Jane and I headed to the markets before finding a store that sold us a beautiful designer luxury handbag, a copy of the expensive original one, and this bag was a perfect copy. We then handed the Chinese man the agreed one hundred yuan. He did not accept my note as he said it was a new note, and when I replied, "I just got it from the nearby ATM," he then showed the note to his Boss, who then, after a quick look at it, handed it back to me.

We were about to leave empty-handed, and then suddenly, the Boss's voice said, "Do you have any other notes?". I then pulled another note from my wallet, and then his face smiled and accepted the second note. It all seemed strange, but at the end of the day, Jane was happy with her new handbag, and I was pleased with how she appreciated my gift.

I understood later in the day what they had done to me. I attempted to spend the note that the handbag seller had returned to me. To my dismay, it was swiftly rejected by the vendor with a raised eyebrow of suspicion. Confusion washed over me as I glanced at Jane, searching for answers. At that moment, our gazes met, and we both realized the truth - we had unwittingly fallen victim to a clever trick.

The handbag seller had cunningly switched the legitimate note with a counterfeit one when our attention was elsewhere. Our innocence had been manipulated; our trust was exploited. Feelings of betrayal mingled with a faint sense of amusement, for it seemed we had stumbled upon yet another lesson in the intricate dance of life. Shaking our heads, we exchanged a knowing glance, silently acknowledging the depth of our naivety.

We spent our last hours in Shenzhen scaling to the one-hundred-and-sixteenth floor of the wondrous Ping An Finance Tower. As the doors of the observation deck opened before us, a breathtaking panorama unfolded, revealing the vast expanse of the city below. Skyscrapers stretch towards the heavens, and the bustling streets below resemble rivers of light, flowing with the energy of millions of souls that call this metropolis home. My mind then drifted back, remembering the words of a Rolling Stones song, "Time waits for no one, and it won't wait for us," as our departure looms upon us.

We then returned to our hotel to organize our bags. Tomorrow would bring a change of scenery, for our ferry awaits to carry us swiftly to the Hong Kong airport. A short thirty-minute journey separates us from the next chapter of our tale - a flight to the narrow streets and hidden gems of Taipei City, Taiwan.

As the sun cast its warm glow upon us, we embarked on a short 90-minute flight to Taoyuan Airport Taipei, our journey unmarred by any untoward incidents. With swift efficiency, we found ourselves aboard a train bound for the heart of this captivating city for two days stopover. Nestled just a stone's throw away from the train station lay the modest yet inviting abode known as Hotel Relax. Its very name seemed to beckon us to heed its advice and embrace the tranquility it promised.

We made our way to the exuberant Young Taipei District with a feeling of youth in our veins. There, amidst the lively bustle, we stumbled upon a perfect, relaxed street barbecue spot. The tantalizing aroma of sizzling skewers filled the air as we indulged in succulent chicken, savory tofu, and earthy mushrooms, accompanied by a few local brews, before bidding farewell to the night for an early sleep.

Dawn greeted us with promises of new adventures, and soon, we found ourselves whisked away on a train to the renowned hot spring district of Beitou. The therapeutic embrace of the 42-degree spring water soothed our aches and pains, easing both body and soul, a sanctuary of peace amidst the bustling city.

Returning to the familiar embrace of the lively street barbecue stall in the evening, we couldn't help but feel a sense of déjà vu, as if the echoes of the previous night lingered in the air, blending into a harmonious symphony of memories.

Our brief stay in Taipei unveiled a world of warmth and hospitality, the locals' friendly demeanor leaving a warm mark upon our hearts. Yet, as we bid farewell to this enchanting city, our thoughts drifted towards the next leg of our odyssey. Then my mind drifted to thinking of our two weeks stopover in Japan en route to Las Vegas for a meeting with King Elvis to tie our knot tight for a life together always.

Chapter 8

Japan.

Now, our hearts were set on a new destination, the land of the rising sun. As the sun began to dip below the horizon, our thoughts already focused on the culture that awaited us in Japan.

We boarded our Eva Air Boeing 787, and in the blink of an eye, we arrived at Narita Tokyo. Actually, it was a two-and-a-half-hour flight. The warm, comforting smile written across Jane's face was all I needed, and no words were spoken. Soon, we were on the Narita Express train on the way to our humble hotel in Shinjuku, and we now began our tour of Tokyo by night with the first stop, the Skytree Tower. Arriving at the top just before sunset, we looked across this busy city from four hundred fifty meters above sea level.

As we explored Tokyo's vibrant streets, I noticed a pained look on Jane's face as we walked back to our hotel, where her secret of a severe knee infection became apparent and was not looking good. I have no idea why she kept it a secret, but after some protests the following morning, we set out in search of a doctor. After a few inquiries, we found a compassionate physician who carefully examined Jane's knee. His diagnosis was sobering, but he prescribed antibiotics and healing cream, assuring us that with time and care, she would recover.

Our afternoon unfolded at a slower pace, but we still marveled at the bustling Shibuya crossing, where a sea of people ebbed and flowed with mesmerizing precision. The Ginza district beckoned with its elegant shops and charming cafes, each moment etching itself into our memories.

As night descended, we returned to our hotel, the weight of the day settling upon our shoulders. Despite the challenges, I found myself grateful for the quiet moments, knowing that even in the face of uncertainty, our journey in Japan held the promise of unexpected beauty and unwavering hope.

Sunrise and a new day dawned with a full-day tour of the majestic Mount Fuji. Our tour guide picked us up at the Love Statue near Shinjuku train station, and we were soon on a bus for a two hours ride, excited to see this world-renowned landmark. It was minus four degrees as we arrived at the summit, looking over the snow-covered peak. Only in summer were people allowed to climb to the top, but Jane and I were content with the view from where we were. The next stop was Lake Ashii, where we arrived by cable car and boarded an old-fashioned boat named Hakone for a picturesque cruise along the calm, tranquil waters. In the fading light, our bus was waiting for us to return to our hotel, a cherished chapter in our Japanese odyssey.

On arrival, we had a twenty-minute walk to our hotel. It was below zero, and my body was not handling the cold so well. The room was cold, and I began to freeze; I did not know what was happening. My hands were shaking out of control, and my body was shivering. Finally in Jane's arm, I found respite and the fatigue of the day's trials giving way to the refreshing embrace of sleep.

Through her unwavering support, the night's bitter cold was no match for warmth, love, and care. Jane covered me with anything warm and hugged me tight until I became regular and finally drifted off to sleep. The warmth of Jane's embrace became my medicine, guiding me back from the brink of hypothermia. As she held me close, the tremors subsided, and a sense of calm seeped through me, soothing the jagged edges of the cold's assault.

I woke early, and luckily, my recovery from hypothermia was complete. Hence, we soon checked out and headed to the Shinkansen Train for a two hours trip south to Osaka, the second largest city in Japan after Tokyo, where we would stay for the next five days. Our hotel was great and had a sauna and onsen, where I spent my night sweating it out and keeping my body temperature high. These kinds of places were common in Japan, and the smiling naked bodies looked content and seemed to be enjoying, and so was I, and what a contrast from last night's frightening experience.

We still had a lot of exploring to do in a short time, so at daybreak, we were on the train to Kyoto, only a thirty-minute ride away. This is an ancient city and the previous capital of Japan from 1794 to 1868. It was the home of the emperor before it was moved to Edu, which was renamed Tokyo. We explored this unique city from the Fushimi-Inari-Taisha Shrine to Kiyomizu-Dera ("Pure Water Temple") we're here on this high peak; we looked over the town and watched the sun descend, holding each other tight and feeling so content with seeing this magical city and all its ancient past.

The next day, as the wheels of the train carried us towards Kobe, memories of 1995 returned to my thoughts when an earthquake devastated the port city with over 6,500 lives lost. There were no visible signs of the earthquake in this picturesque city that offered us a contrast to Kyoto. We arrived back in Osaka early, and it was now a week since Jane had taken her last medicine for her infected knee, so we sat rugged up on the river, drinking cold beer and enjoying the feeling of freedom.

Morning broke, and the train pulled us further south to Hiroshima, just a further 90-minute trip on the Shinkansen. This peaceful place had a sad past when, at 8:15 on August 6, 1945, an atomic bomb devastated the city, taking the lives of over 140,000 innocent people who would have had no idea what happened at the time. Our first stop was the Peace Memorial Park, where we spent hours looking over photos and reading stories, and the realization of the atrocity became very clear.

At night, we found a band playing melodies of Japanese music, and we toasted some beers to help numb the painful memory of the A-bomb. Only two days here in Hiroshima, and on our last day, we visited the temples, shines, and parks of this friendly, peaceful city. Jane and I loved the sightseeing and history of Japan and never rested for even one day, with our romance taking a back seat to history. Tomorrow, we will be on the move again further south to Fukuoka.

Our train pulled in at 2 p.m. so we dropped our bags at the hotel and set out to explore this modern city that merged with Hakata on April 1, 1889. All afternoon and all night, we explored, and then at daybreak, we were on the move with our first stop, Nagasaki, the city where the second atomic bomb was dropped. We did not visit the peace museum here as we decided it would be better to take the cable car to the seaside city's highest peak. The view was out of this world and showed just how magnificent this thriving city was from this peak. We had one more stop on the way back to Fukuoka, and this was to try the Takeo "Motoyu" Onsen, known as the oldest hot spring in Japan, dating back to 1869, and was used for the purifying ritual in the Japanese religion "Shinto."

Jane and I got our Google map directions wrong, and without knowing, we wandered into the wrong place where we were met by an angry Japanese man wielding a Samurai sword and yelling loudly in Japanese with words that did not sound inviting. We were out the door quickly and did not stop running for one hundred meters before stopping to look back and make sure that angry man was nowhere in sight. We both looked at each other and smiled, and we were not really sure if the Samurai man was just trying to scare us or kill us. One thing I do know is I was not going back to say sorry.

We then finally found the hot spring nearby and were soon soaking in 42 degrees water, feeling every bone in our body being soothed. Only two ten-minute soaks were enough as the heat was just bearable but a really fulfilling feeling. I felt the past spirits were watching me soak closely, casting a feeling of contentment and easing my body and soul.

Arriving late back at the hotel, we packed all our things ready for the final stop on our Japanese tour. It was a 90-minute flight to Okinawa onboard our ANA Airlines plane, and our first night in this Japanese version of Hawaii was a party night, we found an Irish pub and sipped on a Guinness, and being the first time for Jane to drink this stout, it was hard work. It was twenty degrees on this island, and we spent our last two days hanging out on the sandy Manza beach.

Our Japanese odyssey had now come to an end, and although our bodies were tired from our two-week tour, we were now ready for Las Vegas. I hugged Jane tight and looked into her eyes as we slept one last night in the land of temples, shrines, and samurai stories full of history and peace.

Chapter 9

Las Vegas (Our Wedding).

The past months in time had similar parallels as a fantasy dream, and the time had delivered me near to the highlight of my life. Like a time capsule I boarded that was a little out of control, but the landing location was here. I was now onboard the Boeing 787 taking me to Las Vegas and soon I would be married to my destiny at Graceland's Chapel by "The King" Elvis Presley, or at least his lookalike impersonator. This was a closely guarded secret I had kept from Jane since I organized it all online when we were in Hong Kong.

The flight ahead stretched out like a vast expanse of time, nearly twelve hours, to be exact. But I was cool, calm, and collected as I settled into my seat with anticipation of what awaited me in Las Vegas, fueling my every breath. Beside me was my soon-to-be wife. Her beauty was radiant even in the dullness of the airplane cabin. At that moment, there was no need for words. Our connection spoke volumes, and together, we set out on this journey of a lifetime. As the hours ticked by, we entertained ourselves in the world of movies, finding captivating stories unfolding before us.

We indulged in the culinary delights offered by the airline. The simple act of sharing a meal brought comfort and warmth, reminding us that even amid grand ventures, it was the small moments of connection that truly mattered.

A few beers found their way into our hands, adding an extra layer of cheer and relaxation. Time seemed to waltz with us, swaying to the rhythm of our laughter and the clinking of glasses. And then, in a blink of an eye, the hours evaporated into thin air. Like sand slipping through the crevices of an hourglass, time moved swiftly, with or without our consent. But in this instance, I wanted it to move fast, to whisk us away to our desired destination, where the culmination of our love story awaited.

For it was there, amidst the marvelous spectacle of Las Vegas, that our journey would reach its zenith. It was there that I would take Jane's hand and lead her down the aisle, where we would exchange vows and start on a new chapter of our lives together. With anticipation, we braced ourselves for the plane's final descent into this legendary city where dreams come to life, where love is celebrated, and where surprises wait to be unveiled.

The bright lights of the Las Vegas Strip illuminated the night sky, casting an otherworldly glow upon the city. Our hotel in Vegas was the Cosmopolitan, which was part of the Marriott that sat silently at the top of the Vegas strip. This place was a legendary strip that I only saw in movies, and just to be here forced me to pinch myself for good measure. I pinched Jane also, and she said, "Ouch! Why did you do that?" I just smiled silently, and maybe Jane got the message as she smiled back and never pushed her question further. Las Vegas is known to the world as the gambling hub of the planet, where fortunes were lost and won twenty-four hours a day and three hundred sixty-five days of the year and, to be correct, three hundred and sixty-six in a leap year. Nearly every show and artist who was somebody played here at some time in their career. Such was the impact of the city that was sitting contentedly in a basin floor of the Mojave Desert surrounded by mountain ranges on all sides.

The night was filled with a sense of mystery as Jane and I stepped into the bustling streets of Las Vegas. Something extraordinary was about to happen, and Jane's curiosity bubbled in her eyes as I hailed a taxi and directed the driver to the Nevada Marriage License Bureau, which was open from 8 a.m. till midnight. We entered the building at 11 p.m. to organize the paperwork. Jane, with a curious smile, then asked, "Why are we here?". I smiled mischievously, my heart pounding with anticipation. "We're registering for our wedding on Thursday." I disclosed, unable to hold back the secret any longer.

Jane's face changed with the biggest smile overtaking her face. No words, just total surprise on her beautiful young face. It was not until we were home, she showed her true feeling of joy, nearing the point of insanity. Jane was happy about this dream plan but a little mad that I kept it a secret.

We discovered one year later that August 16 was the anniversary of the death of King Elvis Presley in 1977, a sad day for all music lovers. It would be doubtful such a talent would ever be seen again, like the King, who is known as a legend. In Las Vegas, there were more Elvis impersonators than anywhere in the United States or, for that matter, anywhere else in our universe.

Just one more day until the wedding, so we did some shopping for our wedding apparel. Jane was easy to please, finding her dream gown at the very first boutique we visited. The dress that she loved was a gorgeous knee-length white gown with lace. Her choice after seeing her wearing this perfect fitting dress made me realize how lucky I was, or as the Ed Sheeran song goes, "I saw her in the dress looking so beautiful," and yes, maybe I do not deserve it, but I wanted her all. She was looking perfect today.

As I gazed at her in awe, a feeling of unworthiness washed over me. How could someone like me be so blessed to have someone so perfect by my side? But despite my doubts, I wanted nothing more than to hold this extraordinary woman and cherish her with all my being. She was my dream come true, and at that moment, she looked and felt like pure perfection. Little did I know that the magic of that dress was only the beginning of the surprises that awaited us on our journey towards forever.

We slept as usual, tightly bonded in each other's arms until morning broke and the sun's rays beamed through the open curtains. We first munched down a simple breakfast and then excitedly went back to the room to prepare for our 2 p.m. wedding.

Downstairs we had no problems in finding a taxi and the driver knew quite well where our destination was located, just a fifteen-minute drive from the hotel. The driver wished us well and was a real joker and put us in a good mood for the day ahead, so I tipped him a ten-dollar note, which was appreciated with a warm thank you. It was almost 2 p.m., but before taking the momentous step towards matrimony, we paused at the front of the chapel, capturing precious photographs that would forever encapsulate the beauty of our sacred union.

In that suspended moment, the world stood still, allowing us to engross ourselves in the profound significance of the day. Every smile, every touch, every glance carried within it the weight of a thousand promises, binding us together in an unbreakable bond. Little did we know, as the shutter clicked, freezing those moments in time, that the surprises and emotions that were yet to unfold would eclipse even our wildest dreams. But in that snapshot, we held the essence of our love, a never-ending story waiting to be written.

With bated breath, we entered this chapel of love, and Jane stood beside me, dressed simply perfect with her white lace gown, her high-heeled silver shoes, and cashmere-like hair that shined like a precious diamond. As for myself, I was dressed in a long-sleeved black shirt and white tie with blue jeans and black snake-skinned shoes. I was with the girl I wanted to spend the rest of my life with, and we both had simple, pure happiness in our souls. It was just me, Jane, the cameraman and Elvis. We realized that our story was not simply ordinary but rather an extraordinary tale of two souls with life and love. And so, with Elvis as our witness, we vowed to dance through life together, embracing the surprises and emotions that lay ahead forever as one in the harmony of our love.

The chapel was adorned with glitz and glamour, its walls echoing the timeless tunes of Elvis Presley. As the music swirled around us, a figure emerged from the shadows, tall and commanding. With a bright gold blazer, jet-black hair, and rings that glistened on every finger, he embodied the spirit of the King himself. For a moment, I imagined this was Elvis himself, but of course, this was not the case, and as I remember, Elvis was not this tall.

Now! Our ceremony began. He walked Jane down the aisle of the chapel to where I was standing at the altar while he was singing his favorite song, "Can't Help Falling in Love." I joined the chorus as he joined our hands. Next, we repeated our vows after Elvis's whist, looking into each other's eyes. Elvis was singing "Love Me Tender," increasing the true loving feelings inside my heart. Only then did I place the ring on Jane's finger, and I said with loving eyes full of affection in my voice. "I promise that I will love you tender," never have a "Suspicious Mind," never will I leave you in "Heartbreak Hotel," and will always be your "Hunka Hunka Burning Love." Jane then placed the ring on my finger and repeated the same vows to me softly and sweetly while tightly squeezing my hand, holding back her tears of joy.

With the blessing from Elvis, we were declared husband and wife. The chapel erupted in applause and cheers, at least the cameraman cheered, celebrating our union. At that moment, time stood still, and the world around us faded into the background. We kissed with love and deep affection as our hearts and eyes were crying with immense happiness. Words could not begin to describe our feelings, and now our promises were sealed. After our vows were made, we danced out of the chapel, singing "Viva Las Vegas."

Many would say this was a corny wedding and not actual. Still, our wedding in this little chapel of love was the most solemn ceremony ever, and our vows, promises, and commitment were more real than any ceremony that was ever made. This was about Jane and me with no acting, no fake vows, only a real deep commitment to be together till our last breath from our bodies was possible.

In front of the chapel, I was approached by the driver of a long white limousine, and he said for fifty dollars, he would give us a ride home to our hotel, which included a glass of French champagne. I agreed without hesitation. Inside the limousine, the air was filled with an aura of elegance. Jane and I sipped on our sweet, chilled drinks, feeling as if we were the King and Queen of the world. The bubbles danced on our tongues, and with each sip, we embraced the boundless possibilities that lay before us.

Arriving at the hotel room, we ordered a bucket of ice and two champagne glasses and then placed our bottle of Moet champagne that we bought for the occasion and made love while the bottle was chilling. Love and desire were the winners as we surrendered ourselves to the intoxicating moment. The room became a sanctuary of pleasure, our connection deepening with every breath. Time seemed to have no meaning as the night transformed into an intimate symphony of love and shared desires.

The hours slipped away, and we remained cocooned in our paradise. The taste of the champagne lingered on our lips, intermingling with the memories of our passion. In the calm moments of the night, we reveled in the knowledge that tomorrow held another rare chance, beckoning us to explore the wonders of the Grand Canyon. As the sun rose on our second day, we held tightly the excitement of our new titles as Mr. and Mrs. Our honeymoon highlight awaited us, and today, it was the majestic Grand Canyon that called our names. With eager hearts, we made our way to the lobby, where our driver greeted us promptly. The radiant joy of being newlyweds filled the air as we embarked on this grand journey together.

Our first stop was the awe-inspiring Hoover Dam, a true marvel of engineering nestled in the Black Canyon of the mighty Colorado River. It was a forty-minute drive to the dam, located near Boulder City. As we approached the site, its monumental presence cast a spell upon us. The Hoover Dam stood tall, proud, and timeless, a testament to human ingenuity and determination. We marveled at its colossal structure, towering two-hundred-and-twenty meters above the river below. Its width, or storage length, stretched an impressive one-hundred-and-eighty kilometers, providing vital water supplies for the luminous city of Las Vegas. The sheer magnitude of this monument left us humbled by the power of human innovation.

As we boarded our van on our onward journey to the celebrated Grand Canyon, we traveled through isolated desert landscapes, where cacti stood proudly, bearing witness to the passage of time. The road stretched before us, leading us closer to this natural wonder. After one hour of driving, we arrived at the rim of the canyon. The sight that greeted us was nothing short of awe-inspiring. Standing side by side, my wife and I gazed upon the vastness before us. The Grand Canyon, once a shallow sea thousands of years ago, now reveals its majestic beauty. It stretched an astonishing four hundred and forty-six kilometers long, with a width of twenty-nine kilometers and an average depth of one thousand eight hundred and twenty-nine meters.

As we took in the breathtaking view, I couldn't help but feel a profound sense of gratitude for the love I shared with my wife. The Canyon's magnificence paled in comparison to the depth of my affection for her. We exchanged a gentle kiss amidst this natural wonder. We ventured onto the glass-bottom walkway, marveling at the dizzying depths beneath us. Peering down, we marveled at the sheer magnitude of the canyon, its bottom barely visible to the human eye. It was as if we were suspended between heaven and earth, caught in a moment of pure wonder.

After spending three hours exploring the grandeur of the Canyon, we feasted on a delicious barbecue lunch, savoring the flavors of the Southwest. Contentment washed over us as we soaked in the memories we had created throughout the day. As we boarded the van for the drive back to the dazzling lights of the Las Vegas Strip, exhaustion settled in. Our hearts were filled with contentment and a deep sense of satisfaction. The day had been remarkable, a testament to the power of love and the beauty of the world we inhabit. We drifted off to sleep, relishing in the blissful contentment that only true happiness can bring.

On our last day in America's playground, we set about on a casino crawl like no other. We wandered through the celebrated halls of Caesars Palace, immersed ourselves in the Venetian's charming canals, and even tried our luck at

Circus Circus and MGM. The atmosphere was electric, filled with the sounds of the clinking of coins.

We found ourselves drawn to the blackjack tables, feeling the thrill of the game as we placed our bets. As luck would have it, fortune smiled upon us, and we walked away with a modest profit of one hundred dollars. The taste of victory was sweet, and our smiles widened as we sipped our complimentary corona beers, savoring the moment of celebration.

As I stood amidst the flashing lights and dazzling displays, I couldn't help but feel a sense of overwhelming positivity. This trip, this dream come true, was not just about the destinations or the experiences. It was about sharing this incredible journey with the one I held most dear. With each passing moment, my anticipation grew for what awaited us in our next chapter - our honeymoon in Hawaii. The promise of pristine beaches, turquoise waters, and magical sunsets beckoned us.

Life had suddenly taken a turn, treating me with a touch of destiny. The sense of being unique, of being truly alive, enveloped me. And as the day came to an end, I couldn't wait to continue this remarkable journey, explore new horizons, and create cherished memories. Tomorrow, when we set foot on the sandy shores of Hawaii, I knew that our love story would unfold in ways we could only dream of. The road ahead was abundant with possibilities. My spirit filled with positivity, and I was ready for this honeymoon of a lifetime.

Chapter 10

Hawaii.

Our Hawaiian Airlines plane was slowly descending on the approach to Honolulu Airport, and gazing out of the window, I could see the swell building in the notorious ocean below. This marked the first day of our extended honeymoon with the travel plans I had written in my diary. I expected this time in our life to be nothing short of remarkable in the coming months. Maybe our honeymoon would be written about like married Marco Polo, such was my high expectations. I then stole a glance at my cute wife close beside me as we landed. She gave me a feeling of contentment that only love can make a person feel.

As the warm Hawaiian breeze caressed our faces, we stepped off the plane, filled with anticipation for our dream honeymoon in paradise. The scent of tropical flowers permeated the air, welcoming us to the enchanting land of sun, sand, and surf. With wide eyes and smiles plastered on our faces, we collected our luggage and hopped into a taxi that took us to our home away from home for the next four days - the Marriott Courtyard Hotel in Waikiki. We were traveling light with only two small suitcases and then after a short ride we arrived. Hawaii is one of the places most people dream of visiting, and we were two of those people.

As we entered the hotel's grand lobby, we were immediately greeted by the friendly staff, who welcomed us with a heartfelt "Aloha." The word carried not only a warm sentiment but also an invitation to enjoy the beauty and spirit of the islands. This was the start of an adventure we had dreamed about for years.

It was nearing sunset, so we walked to the beach tightly holding each other's hands, stopping off at one of the plentiful ABC stores where we were able to find some small bottles of Barefoot red wine made from the famous Napa Valley grapes. We sat on the sands of Waikiki, romancing while watching the glowing sun bid farewell, dipping beneath the horizon. At that moment, a daring spirit ignited within us. Love and the sweet red nectar of the wine urging us to seize this moment of the night. With the beach deserted and the moon as the only witness, we surrendered to the allure of the moment. Our newfound sweet red wine seemed to put us in the mood to be daring as 9 p.m. was approaching. We made love in the sand without caring if anyone was watching and then strolled home with a naughty grin on our faces to the comfort of our room.

Wrapped in each other's arms, contentment washing over us, we drifted into a deep slumber. The whispers of the ocean lulled us while dreams of our honeymoon danced in our heads. We slept well without worrying about the sand all through the bed sheets that our bodies delivered from the beach.

With the first rays of daybreak painting the sky with gold and pink, we eagerly boarded a van that we had booked for a full-day excursion around the island. Our journey began in the serene mountainous hills, where lush forests adorned the landscape. The air was filled with the sweet scent of wildflowers, carrying promises of hidden treasures waiting to be discovered.

As the van ascended higher into the mountains, our guide beckoned us to look out the windows, pointing towards two majestic peaks looming in the distance. "Behold," he said, his voice filled with reverence, "the mighty guardians of this island, the twin volcanoes that shaped this magnificent land." The van continued its journey, winding through picturesque coastal roads that overlooked pristine beaches kissed by turquoise waves. We both gazed at the cascading waterfalls that tumbled down the mountainsides, filling the air with a gentle mist that danced in the sunlight.

We pulled up to Sunset Beach, and excitement rippled through the passengers like a wave building momentum. The beach was alive with electric energy, the sound of crashing waves and the cheers of onlookers filling the air. With a heart full of anticipation, I couldn't resist the allure of the pumping surf any longer. It had been a decade since I last rode a board, but the call of the ocean was too strong to ignore. I rented a surfboard, feeling a mix of nerves and adrenaline coursing through my veins.

Paddling out into the vast expanse of the cerulean sea, I was amazed at the power and beauty of the waves that unfolded before me. Expert surfers carved their way across the wave faces with inspiring grace, their movements a breathtaking dance between man and nature. Sitting atop my board, I watched as the champions effortlessly navigated the walls of water, displaying a mastery of the ocean that left me humbled. Their every maneuver was executed with precision, and their connection with the water is evident in every stroke.

Summoning the courage buried deep within me, I positioned myself for my first wave. The rush of adrenaline intensified as I paddled into position, feeling the surge of energy propelling me forward. With a burst of determination, I took off, dropping down the face of the wave. In that electrifying moment, time ceased to exist. The world faded away, leaving only me and the power of the ocean. I turned my board up into the crest of the wave, feeling the sheer exhilaration as it carried me with incredible speed.

I took off on about eight waves, with half of them dumping me while the other half, I made the drop and turned up into the crest of these fast, clean waves. What an experience it was to be out at the world-known surf location riding on my backhand across a perfect right-hand wave. But just as quickly as the moment had arrived, it slipped away. The calls from my fellow travelers snapped me back to reality, reminding me that our adventure was far from over. With a mix of reluctance and gratitude, I paddled back to shore, my heart still pounding with the thrill of the surf.

As I dried off, a renewed sense of possibility filled my spirit. The taste of those perfect waves lingered on my lips, serving as a reminder that sometimes, in the most unexpected moments, we find ourselves capable of incredible feats. And so, with a smile on my face and gratitude in my heart, I rejoined my fellow explorers, forever carrying the spirit of those breathtaking waves within me.

We continued on a thrilling tour as we parked our van near the legendary Banzai Pipeline. The name itself spoke volumes about the danger and excitement that awaited us at this world-renowned surf spot. From a distance, the waves resembled large round pipes, their power evident as they crashed onto the shallow coral reef. It was a sight to behold. As we approached the shoreline, we were astounded by the daredevils who fearlessly rode the left-hand waves with unparalleled skill and bravery. The tube riders, as they were affectionately called, carved through the water with grace and precision, their bodies becoming one with the immense power of the ocean. It was a mesmerizing display of courage and determination, leaving us in awe at their abilities.

Our next stop was Waimea Bay, where the waves only appeared a few times a year, and today happened to be one of those days. The sheer size of the waves towering over twenty feet in height. The bay was teeming with adrenaline-seeking surfers, both young and brave, who had come to conquer the perils that this location presented. Known as the birthplace of big wave riders, Waimea Bay held a magnetic pull for those seeking to test their limits. The surfers paddled out with unwavering determination, knowing that the immense swells could easily swallow them whole. It was a place where legends were made, where the line between triumph and disaster was razor-thin.

As we watched the surfers take on the colossal waves, we couldn't help but feel a mixture of admiration and a touch of trepidation. Their commitment to pushing the boundaries of what was deemed possible in the realm of surfing was genuinely remarkable.

Leaving the bay behind, we carried the memories of this day's happenings in our hearts. The sights and sounds of the mighty waves crashing upon the shore and the energy and bravery of the surfers, are all etched into our minds forever. It was a day filled with anticipation, amazement, and a reminder of the indomitable spirit of those who dare to chase their wildest dreams, even in the face of nature's awe-inspiring power. We covered this volcanic island far and wide and after eight hours we were back at our hotel to once again head to the beach and watch the sunset with our newfound friend Barefoot. An early night's sleep was our plan, as tomorrow was a trip that we organized to see Pearl Harbour.

In the early morning light, the warmth of the Hawaiian sun washed over us as we prepared ourselves for a day filled with reflection of a past catastrophe. Our destination was Pearl Harbor, a place that bore witness to a devastating event that forever altered the course of World War II. The memory of that fateful day in 1941 hung heavy in the air when the tranquility of a Sunday morning was shattered by a surprise air strike orchestrated by the Imperial Japanese Navy Air Service.

With a mixture of sadness and curiosity, we ventured into the war museums, stepping back in time to an era filled with bravery, sacrifice, and resilience. Each exhibit unveiled stories of heroism and heartbreak, bringing the past to life before our very eyes. But it was atop the USS Arizona that the true magnitude of the tragedy unfolded before us. Standing on the deck of this iconic battleship, gazing upon its submerged hull where over one thousand lives were lost, a profound sense of reverence enveloped us. It was a haunting reminder of the human toll exacted by war, where the fallen heroes of that day lay entombed even now.

Our final day in Hawaii took an unexpected turn when we were presented with a tempting offer by the front desk attendant at our hotel. A free day at the luxurious Ko Olina resort, complete with a delicious lunch, sounded too good to pass up. The only catch was that we had to endure a ninety-minute timeshare presentation. Intrigued and eager for an adventure, we agreed, secretly thrilled to be granted access to a world typically reserved for the wealthy. As we stepped foot onto the resort grounds, we were immediately taken by this atmosphere of luxury. The private beach beckoned us, its crystal-clear waters inviting us to dive in and savor the last moments of our Hawaiian getaway. We swam, lounged under the warm sun, and marveled at the beauty that surrounded us.

The highlight of our day came in the form of a mesmerizing hula show. As the dancers gracefully moved their hips to the rhythm of pounding drums, we were captivated by their talent. The energy of the performance electrified the air, leaving us with admiration for the rich cultural heritage that Hawaii possessed.

It was a remarkable day and a memorable trip to Hawaii, but we still had one last sunset to share with our dear friend red wine Barefoot. As the evening approached, we made our way to our favorite spot on the beach to witness the breathtaking sunset. With the sun sinking below the horizon, we strolled back to our hotel, hand in hand, the memories of our remarkable day at Ko Olina swirled in our minds.

It was an unexpected adventure filled with surprises, beauty, and the joys of friendly encounters. As the waves gently lapped against the shore, we reveled in the magic of our Hawaiian escapade, cherishing the moments that would forever hold a special place in our hearts. As we slept, our minds started to focus on our next stop, Los Angeles, California.

Chapter 11

L.A and San Diego.

The landing approach at Los Angeles International Airport was a new experience as I was looking out the plane window and I could see another plane coming into land side by side with us. The dual landing was exciting once I overcame the shock of seeing another plane so close, and soon, we touched down at Tom Bradley International Airport. We stayed downtown, only a thirty-minute Uber ride from the airport. Jane and I were gazing at the sights and sounds of this unique and colorful city.

Our hotel, the luxurious JW Marriott, welcomed us with open arms. It stood tall amidst the cityscape, offering a stunning view of the bustling downtown below. We settled into our lavish room, feeling like royalty as we took in the elegant surroundings. So here we were in the city that was known for its movie stars and swimming pools, ready to explore, and we were excited as we slept in the land of the rich and famous. This was also the home of playboy millionaire Hugh Hefner, known as maybe the luckiest man in the world.

Morning in Los Angeles, ready to undertake new locations, and after indulging in a delicious breakfast, our hearts filled with the desire to explore the iconic Santa Monica Beach. We hopped on the metro with spirits high, eager to soak in the flamboyant atmosphere that awaited us.

Stepping onto the sandy shores, a wave of energy washed over me. Santa Monica Beach was a haven of endless possibilities. With its lively boardwalk, inviting eateries, and boundless entertainment, it was indeed a playground for the senses. To thoroughly soak me in the beachside charm, we decided to hire a push bike built for two called a tandem, and "I could see my honey in the rear-view mirror." Her smile could launch a rocket ship, and she looked sexy in her tight white shorts, making my mind continually visit the gutter with my naughty thoughts.

We arrived at Venice Beach; wow, this place was like you see in the movies with cool hippy-like Californians selling all that was possible and mostly legal. However, I noticed the strong smell of an illegal substance filling the clear, cool air mixed with the salt spray from the ocean waters. On the sands, there were tall blonde and brunette girls and muscled bound men. I guess all dreamed of being discovered by the talent scouts in this place of dreams and imagined that someone was watching them and, hopefully, they would be found.

The beach was a happening place, with beach volleyball games being played all day long. Jane and I watched the games for a short passage of time. These game participants were good-looking with magnificent physique people. There were, on the other side, many hippies who seemed to be in a world of their own and had no desire to be discovered, especially by the police. All in all, these Californians blended well like a melting pot.

We were back on the bike, heading back to Santa Monica Pier. It was now mid-afternoon, and we noticed a Bubba Gump restaurant at the front of the pier, so we dropped back our colorful bike. Before lunch, we strolled to the end of this long timber pier, watching all kinds of variety acts and buskers entertaining the willing crowd. At piers end, we both threw coins into the Pacific Ocean, feeling our wishes were already written in the stars for all stargazers to see. After this, our smiling faces were soon in Bubba Gumps, eating what this restaurant was known for. This restaurant was made from concepts from the 1994 movie Forrest Gump, with Tom Hanks, the leading actor in the movie, playing the part that won him an Oscar for his role. Here, we ate fresh shrimp, feeling contented with our day's activities.

As the day came to a close, we knew that our journey in Los Angeles had uncovered a world of surprises, emotions, and unspoken desires. With hearts brimming with memories of laughter, flirtation, and a touch of mischief, we vowed to continue weaving stories together, living the next chapter of our story. We slept well this night, resting early, ready for another L.A. day once our eyes opened tomorrow.

Morning broke with the sunshine beaming into our room in Southern California, and the song says it never rains here, and these were true words sung in the Albert Hammond song of the early seventies. We were out and about in this amazing city where celebrities and actors could be spotted about town trying their best to be as inconspicuous as possible, or they would be forced to sign autographs for long periods. Some wanted to be spotted and appreciated the fuss of adoring fans.

We traveled from Beverley Hills to the Hollywood Walk of Fame, where the imprints of past greats adorned the sidewalk. Handprints preserved in cement served as tributes to the unforgettable icons that had once graced the silver screen. We paused at each star, their fingers tracing the names of legends like Marilyn Monroe and John Wayne, paying homage to the pioneers who paved the way for future generations.

We had tickets to the legendary Hollywood Bowl; nightfall descended, casting a mystical aura over the amphitheater nestled at the foot of the majestic Hollywood Hills. Anticipation buzzed in the air as the crowd eagerly awaited the arrival of music legend Steely Dan. The atmosphere was electrified. A wave of excitement was buzzing through the audience. The rhythmic beats and soulful melodies resonated through nightfall descending upon the legendary Hollywood Bowl, casting a mystical aura over the open-air venue. As the band took the stage, an explosion of sound erupted, engulfing the night with a symphony of timeless classics.

Despite the passing of time, the musicians exuded an energy that defied their age. They poured their hearts into each note, transporting concertgoers back to an era when their music first graced the airwaves. Amidst the musical euphoria, the scent of marijuana wafted through the air, adding an extra layer of hazy nostalgia to the evening. Beers were raised in celebration as laughter and joy mingled with the harmonies echoing across the Hollywood Bowl.

Our trip home from Hollywood to Downtown Los Angeles on the metro was one incident with many homeless people onboard. Most were sleeping, but one pulled a knife and waved his weapon recklessly, demanding money from the passengers. His eyes were staring towards me, not sure if I was his target. I could see this man was desperate, and it seemed he would do almost anything to satisfy his need for whatever drug he required to satisfy his body. Maybe the heroine now owned this man's soul, and why he took this path in life I did not question. I had almost one hundred and eighty dollars in my wallet and placed it on the carriage floor, which he snatched in desperation and then jumped off the metro at the next stop. We were both very shaken, and I realized nighttime was not safe onboard this train, but luckily, we arrived at the stop near our hotel downtown in one piece and without any knife or gunshot wounds.

On our last day in Los Angeles, we walked the Hollywood Hills. It was a challenging, hot, steep walk with the hot L.A. sun above showing no mercy. All the while keeping our eyes peeled as we stepped carefully, hoping not to meet up with a rattlesnake that inhabited these hills. The Hollywood sign loomed overhead, a symbol of dreams and aspirations guiding our way. Three arduous hours passed as we finally emerged from our trek, arriving at the Space Observatory at the sight of a famous scene in the 1955 movie "Rebel without a Cause" starring the legend James Dean. At night, we were buzzing after some memorable days in L.A. ready for our morning three-hour Amtrak train trip to our next stop, which would be the city of San Diego.

Morning dawned, and we found ourselves at the bustling Amtrak station, awaiting the next chapter of our journey. San Diego beckoned, promising new experiences yet to be discovered. As we boarded the train, mingled with the echoing whispers of the Hollywood dreams we left behind.

The wheels hummed rhythmically as the train carved its path through the scenic landscapes, carrying us toward the next chapter. The wind whispered secrets through the open windows, with salty ocean breezes. Our souls danced with excitement, eager to immerse ourselves into the sprightly San Diego. Los Angeles faded into the distance, leaving memories and our hearts filled with gratitude for the moments shared, the challenges overcome, and the unknown that awaited us just around the bend as the train snaked its way toward San Diego. With every passing mile, we farewelled the shadows of the Hollywood Hills and started on a journey illuminated by the spirit of adventure.

Arriving in San Diego, we eagerly dropped our bags at the Sheraton Four Points, ready to yield ourselves to the lively energy of the city. As dusk began to paint the sky, we made our way to the Gaslamp District. The area was a hub of entertainment, and culture welcomed us with its charm. Music filled the air as people gathered in buoyant restaurants and bars. We found a cozy spot, drawn to the melodic sounds of an acoustic guitarist and singer serenading the crowd. Sipping on cold corona beers, we basked in the warm ambiance, the music caressing our souls. Love songs drifted through the night, combining with the whispers of our hearts. We held each other, cherishing the moments, stealing sweet kisses when the melodies evoked memories of our own love story.

In the upbeat atmosphere of the Gaslamp District, time stood still. We reveled in the simple joy of being together, creating our version of a modern-day Romeo and Juliet. For in our world, our love was not destined for tragedy but for everlasting happiness. As the night wore on, the stars twinkled above us; we danced in the moonlit street, the echoes of the guitar filling our steps with rhythm and grace. Every touch and every smile spoke volumes, giving a warm feeling of love, romance, and shared dreams.

Up early at daybreak and after a light breakfast and a gym workout, we were out to see what we could see. Our first destination was the USS Midway, a magnificent aircraft carrier transformed into a museum. Stepping aboard, we traveled back in time to the devastation that this colossal vessel had witnessed. Next, we made our way to the statue of the kissing soldier, an iconic symbol of victory and peace. As we stood before it, we couldn't help but be moved by the sheer emotion captured in that frozen moment. Inspired by the end of World War II, we shared a tender kiss of our own, grateful for the peace that was bestowed upon the world, knowing that this historical event changed countless lives forever.

In the afternoon, we found ourselves on Coronado Island, drawn to the pristine shores in front of the majestic Hotel Del Coronado. The sparkling waters beckoned us to take the plunge, and we happily obliged. With each splash, we reveled in the simple joys of life, savoring the freedom that comes with liberation from conflict. As the sun began its descent towards the horizon, we watched in wonder. It was as if the heavens themselves were commemorating the triumphs of the past and illuminating the path toward a brighter future.

We bid farewell to the island and returned to our hotel for a well-deserved rest. Tomorrow held promises of further exploration as we planned to visit Tijuana. But for now, as we drifted off to sleep, memories of the USS Midway, the statue of the kissing soldier, and the sun-kissed beaches of Coronado Island were vivid in our dreams.

The Mexican border was a short trolley ride from town, and we had no problems crossing the Mexican border to visit this chaotic town named Tijuana. This place was a little run down and a very unorganized place. It was amazing to think only thirty minutes away was a clean, organized city, and yet here was the opposite, with chaos all around.

Amongst the chaos, we stumbled upon hidden gems that defied explanation. Alleyways filled with street art that spoke volumes, murals depicting the struggles and triumphs of a community determined to thrive. But it was at the border crossing that we truly understood the longing for something more. As we stood in line for hours, waiting to return to the United States, we witnessed the desperation and determination written on the faces of those seeking a better life. The sacrifices made to escape poverty and seize opportunities became all too real.

When we finally got back to San Diego, we decided to submerge ourselves in the Italian neighborhood known as Little Italy. We savored the spaghetti with its rich sauces, washing it down with sweet red wine and transporting us to Rome for one night.

As our journey came to an end, we carried with us a newfound appreciation for the contrasts that exist in the world. From the bravery and heroism of naval warfare on the USS Midway to the poignant symbol of the kissing soldier, from the sun-kissed beaches of Coronado Island to the chaotic charm of Tijuana, and finally, the flavors of Little Italy in San Diego - each experience reminded us of the resilience, hopes and dreams that bind humanity together. Tomorrow, we would be on a bus to Long Beach, where we would set sail on a one-week cruise through Baja, California.

Chapter 12

Queen Mary and Baja California

The honeymooners were traveling on a Greyhound bus for a four-hour ride to Long Beach. As the bus rolled along the highway toward our destination, anticipation filled the air. We were embarking on a week-long journey, ready to set sail on a cruise through the warm waters of Baja California. But before we boarded our ship, we couldn't resist the allure of the majestic Queen Mary.

Gazing up at the imposing vessel, parked gracefully by the harbor, it was hard to believe that this marvel had once dominated the high seas. The Queen Mary, a floating testament to opulence and grandeur, had captivated the hearts of countless travelers throughout its storied voyages. It was parked here after its last trip from Southampton on October 31, 1967. It now serves as a tourist attraction and a floating hotel. A real trip back in time on this luxury ship, which was built by the same people that built the ill-fated Titanic but was forty-two meters longer.

Stepping onboard, we were transported back in time. The polished woodwork and elegant furnishings exuded a timeless charm, beckoning us to explore every corner of this floating masterpiece. As we wandered through its corridors and lounges, we couldn't help but imagine the famous faces that once graced these very halls. Movie stars like Elizabeth Taylor and Clark Gable had strolled these decks, their glamorous presence adding a touch of Hollywood magic to the ship's already illustrious reputation. Bob Hope had entertained crowds with his signature wit, while dignitaries such as Winston Churchill and General Dwight Eisenhower had experienced the unparalleled luxury that the Queen Mary offered.

Leaving the Queen Mary, we made our way to the boarding gate of the Carnival Panorama cruise liner for our seven-day cruise. This boat was luxurious, and our room was perfect and cozy. Soon, the horns blew loudly, and we set sail while sitting on the top deck drinking champagne on ice. I was on top of the world, looking over the calm ocean and watching a mesmerizing sunset with my wife and lover, realizing life cannot get any better than this.

Life has a way of surprising us, weaving unexpected gifts into the fabric of our existence. And so, instead of questioning or analyzing, I chose to take hold of the beauty of the present. A smile graced my lips, watching the setting sun as I soaked in the abundance of love, joy, and sheer wonder, with my eyes calmly stealing glances at my wife, Jane.

We indulged in endless entertainment onboard, being entertained with live music and captivating stage shows while relishing the abundance of delectable cuisine. On day three, we arrived at Puerto Vallarta. As we disembarked from the cruise ship, our senses were awakened by the calm energy of this sleepy beach resort. With the sun shining brightly, we couldn't resist the allure of the crystal-clear waters that beckoned us to a secluded beach. After a refreshing swim, we found ourselves surrendering to the hands of young Mexican senoritas, who skillfully eased away all tension with their soothing massages. Oh, the happy ending, a delightful surprise that brought a mischievous grin to my face.

Feeling utterly relaxed and rejuvenated, we returned to our floating home, eagerly awaiting the next stop on our cruise: Mazatlán, Mexico. This city accepted us with open arms, offering a myriad of wonders to explore. For hours on end, we strolled through the streets, captivated by the audacious cliff divers entertaining the eager tourists. But it was a street, seemingly ordinary yet filled with the spirit of an era gone by, that truly captured our hearts. A street adorned with vibrant murals and, of all things, a replica of the iconic Cavern Club where the Beatles once graced the stage. We were sent back in time to a time of nostalgia and a musical revolution.

Once inside this iconic Cavern Club replica, we encountered a group of lively Mexican girls with their infectious laughter and spirits untamed. We shared stories as their company injected a burst of joy into our day. I found myself excitedly watching Jane drinking shots of Tequila with the pretty Mexican senoritas. Soon enough, the flirting began, and Jane let her inhibitions drift away with her hands wandering in the curves and contours of the Mexican girls. With a gentle touch, they all became intoxicated with their laughter and warmth. Happiness engulfed my face as I saw the true Jane let her hair down and throw away her shyness out the nearby window. Her lust for the senoritas also showed passion in their eyes that made them explore the freedom we all desired.

Time slipped away, and we reluctantly bid them farewell. Being teased by Jane, the Mexican girls insisted on keeping in touch and gave their contact details, with promises of a future reunion. As we made our way back to the ship, a tempting thought crossed my mind - what if we stayed? What if we surrendered to the temptation of another day in this exciting Mexican town, embracing the allure of those pretty Mexican beauties? But duty called, and with a mix of reluctance and anticipation, we reluctantly boarded the ship, carrying with us the memories of a day filled with laughter and the promise of what could have been.

And as we sailed away, the moonlit waves shimmering beneath us, our hearts yearning for the unknown that awaited us in the days to come. As the cruise ship made its final stop in the luxurious city of Cabo San Lucas, Mexico, we found ourselves amidst a world of opulence. This up-market waterfront city, where the Pacific Ocean meets the Sea of Cortez, exuded an air of affluence as if it were inhabited only by the wealthy and privileged.

With the sun shining brightly overhead, we couldn't resist the calling of the blue ocean. Like two carefree school kids, we frolicked in the warm waters, playing and splashing with innocent abandon. It was a day of simple fun, a perfect end to our voyage. All good things must come to an end, and we reluctantly boarded the ship for our final day at sea. Determined to keep ourselves healthy and rejuvenated, we dedicated our time to the ship fitness center, preparing our bodies for any future escapades that lay ahead.

As the ship sailed towards its destination, our hearts were a mixture of sadness and excitement, for we were leaving behind our vessel that had provided us with entertainment, comfort, and endless discoveries for the past seven days. It was time to bid farewell to this floating sanctuary and travel new journeys, much like the great merchant explorer Mr. Marco Polo of the 13th century.

Chapter 13

San Francisco

Arriving early in the morning back in Long Beach, we farewelled the ship with a bittersweet feeling in our hearts. Still, the spirit of exploration burned within us, urging us to keep moving forward, seek new locations, and new experiences. Today, we would catch a bus for our next journey from Los Angeles to Bakersfield before boarding the Amtrak Train for a four-and-a-half-hour trip to San Francisco.

We arrived pretty late at night at the city, and its Golden Gate opened up graciously and let us in. This city in the 60s encouraged the young to wear flowers in their hair and promoted free love. It was cold on arrival and reminded me of the saying by Mark Twain, "The coldest winter I ever spent was a summer in San Francisco."

Finally, after a long walk, we found ourselves at Fisherman's Wharf, where the Marriott Hotel awaited us like a sanctuary for weary travelers. Exhausted from a day filled with long miles of travel, we collapsed onto the plush beds, feeling contented and satisfied with our journey. We slept soundly, oblivious to the stories that whispered through the streets, stories of dreamers and artists of innovators and rebels. And as the sun rose over the horizon, we stirred from our contented rest, ready to discover the Golden Gate City that awaited us.

With renewed energy and an eager spirit, we stepped out into the bustling streets, ready to explore the hippy culture, the iconic landmarks, and the undeniable charm that made San Francisco a place like no other. On our first day in San Francisco, we decided to plunge ourselves into the charm of Fisherman's Wharf. We strolled along the water's edge, breathing in the salty air and admiring the picturesque views. Our hunger led us to a cozy little spot where we relished the delicious clam chowder, savoring every spoonful while watching the seagulls dance above the shimmering bay.

The following day, renting two push bikes, we pedaled our way along the water's edge, taking in the breathtaking sights that San Francisco had to offer. After a challenging climb, we found ourselves atop the magnificent Golden Gate Bridge. The wind tousled our hair as we marveled at the iconic structure stretching out before us. With determination and a sense of accomplishment, we rode across to the other side and then back, fulfilling a long-held dream from our never-ending bucket list.

Eager to explore more of the city's rich history, we hopped on the last manually operated cable car in the world. As it rattled and clanged along the tracks, we felt taken back in time, connecting with the bygone era of San Francisco. The cable car took us through the charming streets and colorful neighborhoods, eventually leading us to the lively Castro Street in the heart of the city's gay district.

As night fell upon Castro Street, the atmosphere became electric as we entered a gay bar. We were welcomed, and no one cared if we were gay or not as Jane and I joined the liberated and joyful crowd, dancing to the infectious rhythms of a unique group of talented musicians. The music pulsated through the air, filling us with an over-whelming sense of freedom and unity. We were greeted by the open-minded and accepting community that called this district their own, celebrating life and love in every beat of the music.

In that moment, surrounded by laughter and pure happiness, we realized that San Francisco was not just a city but a place that forever changed the lives of those who experienced it. It was a city of dreams, where freedom reigned and where every individual could be their most authentic self. We left the district that night with hearts full of gratitude and a promise to never forget the profound impact of the high-spirited souls we encountered. San Francisco, with its stunning landmarks, its rich cultural heritage, and its warm-hearted people, has woven itself into the fabric of our memories forever. And as we continued our journey through this captivating city, there was plenty more to surprise us.

On our final day in San Francisco, we visited the infamous Alcatraz Island. It stood like a solitary sentinel, two kilometers from the city shore. As we stepped foot on this eerie isle, we couldn't help but feel a shiver run down our spines. This was no ordinary place. It was once a federal prison, a fortress that housed some of the most notorious criminals of its time. As we walked through the prison walls, we were surrounded by a sense of captivity and despair. The cells stood as silent witnesses to the lives that were once held within their cold, unforgiving walls. In this maximum-security facility, men like Al Capone, George "Machine Gun" Kelly, and Robert Stroud, known as the Birdman of Alcatraz, had once served their sentences. The stories of their crimes hung heavy in the air, reminding us of the darkness that once prevailed here.

We explored every nook and cranny, hoping to catch a glimpse of the past. We felt the weight of solitude that must have plagued the inmates trapped in this living hell on earth. The harshness of the environment, both physical and psychological, permeated our very being. Only the toughest could survive in this unforgiving sanctuary or perhaps even emerge stronger than they had ever been before. As we bid farewell to Alcatraz, we were fortunate to have experienced this glimpse into a world that existed decades ago. It made us appreciate the freedom we often take for granted. Our hearts were filled with deep respect for those who had endured and fought against the darkness, leaving their unique mark on this desolate island.

That night, as we lay in our beds, sleep eluded us. The anticipation of our next stop played in our minds. "The Big Apple" New York City awaited us with its energy and endless possibilities. We dreamt of towering skyscrapers, bustling streets, and a city that never slept.

San Francisco had captivated our hearts, but now it was time to swing to the rhythm of New York. We drifted off to sleep, knowing that tomorrow would bring new surprises and emotions. Our hearts were filled with an unyielding thirst for exploration and a desire to create lasting memories in the city that never ceased to amaze us. Little did we know what marvels awaited us on the other side of the country as our journey continued, engraving itself deeper into our adventurous souls.

Chapter 14

New York.

We were now on the ground at JFK Airport, named after the 35th President of the United States, John F Kennedy, until he was assassinated in Dallas, Texas, on the 22nd of November 1963. We were able to find our van pickup stop to take us to our hotel located close to Times Square, which was the popular entertainment hub in the neighborhood of Broadway. New York, "The Big Apple," was a vast, busy city constantly in motion, never taking a rest.

At the hotel, we were able to book a walking tour for 10 a.m. to show us around on foot and give a little background from a local New Yorker's perspective. Our guide, a true-blue New Yorker with a thick accent and an infectious enthusiasm for his city, led us through the bustling streets. We met near Little Italy in the lower part of Manhattan, where all the streets are lined with restaurants serving Italian dishes on red-and-white checkered tablecloths. As we strolled through the concrete jungle, he wove tales of New York's rich past. From the early days of waves of immigrants seeking a better life, the city had seen it all. It became clear that this was a place where dreams were both forged and shattered, where opportunity and hardship coexisted in a delicate balancing act.

As we walked among the crowds, the city pulsated with energy. Street performers filled the atmosphere with music. The scent of hotdogs and pretzels permeated the air, tempting us to indulge in the quintessential New York's street food experience. With stories of prominent New Yorkers, their triumphs, and their struggles, we learned about the visionaries who shaped the city's skyline, the artists who captured its essence on canvas, and the ordinary people whose resilience defined New York's spirit.

The Big Apple was more than just concrete and steel. It was a melting pot of cultures, ideas, and dreams. It embraced diversity and celebrated individuality. As the tour drew to a close, we found ourselves standing at the edge of Central Park. The vast expanse of green offered a respite from the urban chaos that surrounded us. At that moment, we realized that New York was a city of contrasts found amidst the chaos, where dreams could flourish against all odds. With admiration and gratitude, we bid farewell to our guide. We ventured into the park, eager to explore its hidden corners and discover even more of what this incredible city had to offer. New York welcomed us, inviting us to become part of its story.

The next day, we rode the hop-on hop-off bus, stopping at the Wall Street District. The 9/11 monument where the Twin Towers were hit by hijacked planes piloted by terrorists flying into the buildings on the 11th of September 2001, killing thousands of innocent people seemingly in the name of God. A sad day in the history of not only this majestic city but the whole world; stood in total disbelief on that day in time.

We then rode a ferry to Liberty Island in New York Harbor. Panoramic views of the Statue of Liberty and the vast New York Skyline were also clearly visible from the harbor ferry. This copper statue was a gift from the people of

France. The statue is a figure of Libertas, the Roman goddess of liberty, holding a torch high in her right hand. We were buzzing, and a little pinch of Jane's bum was already known as a test to see if I was dreaming. My wife smiled and said, "No! You're not dreaming, and my bum has a red mark now to prove it". I smiled and held her hand tight as we gazed with amazement at the beauty of the statue and the New York Harbor.

Then, the afternoon was upon us, and we were now at the top of the Empire State Building, where we could look across this magnificent city from a different angle, with its buildings reaching high above the earth and growing towards the sun. This engineering masterpiece was also where the final scenes of the movie "Sleepless in Seattle" were filmed. Maybe this movie was one of the most celebrated happy endings in love story annals.

Jane and I had a grand touring day together and were inseparable as usual, kissing and being contented with each other's company the whole day long. We slept well even with full stomachs after eating a legendary New York pizza cooked in an old-fashioned stone-fired oven with mozzarella cheese and delicious crust inspiring our taste buds. The New Yorkers' accent was unique, but with wide-opened ears, we were able to converse with the locals.

Tomorrow had arrived, and this day, we tortured ourselves in the hotel gym with yesterday's pizza churning in our stomachs. It was now nightfall, and we excitedly headed up to Central Park, just a twenty-minute walk from our hotel, for a loud, deafening concert by John Bon Jovi. The New Yorkers had returned home. Jon Bon Jovi sang with all his heart and soul, his powerful voice reaching the far corners of the park as we swayed with the music, lost in the moment. The band gave their best for over three hours. It was a performance like no other, leaving us stunned. We left the park that night, feeling changed and moved by the experience. It was something we would never forget.

This majestic park was the perfect setting, and the performance could only be described by words that were still not invented in the English language. You could say it was a good concert, but that word was not enough. The words that I could say were "mind-blowing" or even go as far as saying hallucinatory to the point of mind-altering.

Our final concluding day in this city was spent hanging out at Times Square and a little twist to the song "We are leaving tomorrow, not today." This was the very place where images of the legend James Dean were taken back in 1955. These photo images are still seen today on posters and helped launch the career of the then-novice actor.

On our last night, we were on Broadway with tickets to watch the old musical Miss Saigon, and as they say in the classics, it was something old, but oh! it was good. This stage musical is the best I have seen. It is based on the opera Madam Butterfly and similarly tells the tragic tale of a doomed romance of an Asian woman abandoned by her American lover. This performance had it all, with singing, drama, and comedy thrown in, and we left the theatre touched with emotion and teary-eyed. Love can have a tragic ending, and this stage show gives another example of a forbidden fruit of love.

Back in the hotel, we slept as I held Jane close in my arms. Tomorrow morning, we had a flight to New Orleans with our honeymoon that was never-ending, and anyway, why not make it last as long as possible?

Life is far too short, they say, so keeping this in mind, I wanted to spend every minute possible with my wife Jane and see as much as we could see in the time that we possessed to continue of our romantic travel.

Chapter 15

New Orleans.

So here we were in New Orleans, Louisiana, an individual city on the Mississippi River in the Gulf of Mexico. Jane and I were excited to see the jazz musicians and brass bands and party our hardest after being a little conservative in New York. In life, sometimes we need to take it easy and relax, allowing our minds and souls to have a rest. This was not the place to relax but to listen to great music that was still being inspired by the great Louis Armstrong "Satchmo" even though he had passed away more than fifty years ago in 1971. His memory lives on in this funky town, and even the airport is honored in his name.

Excited to hear the jazz music, we wasted no time and approached Bourbon Street, the most happening street in this Cajun-flavored town, which is just a ten-minute walk from our hotel. We could hear the music playing, and our excitement was high. It was 7 p.m., and we were soon in a bar sipping on a couple of Bud beers. The band was playing lively, and they were full of enthusiasm and full of energy, making our heads move to the music while looking around at everyone smiling and moving their feet.

Before long, Jane was sampling the local cocktail called grenades served in, crazy enough, a grenade-shaped container. A couple of these, and Jane was aroused and touching me on the dance floor. No one cared, and we both were hot for each other. Jane looked deep into my eyes, grabbed my hand, and started kissing me as she guided me to the ladies' toilet. Soon, we were in the cubicle with the hardest part of my body inserted inside Jane as she was bent over, holding onto the sink, hoping she would not pull it from the wall. The noise we were making was loud, and after we reached a climax, we just straightened ourselves up and walked nonchalantly back inside the bar like nothing had happened. Even the other ladies in the toilets did not care and only seemed a little surprised but just gave a grin and kept silent. What a naughty thing we did inside the cubical, but sometimes it is good to be daring and crazy.

I ordered two more grenades, and we were swaying both from the cocktails and the music of the jazz band. I noticed an American lady smiling at me and Jane. I invited her to join us as she seemed to be alone. I recognized her from the ladies' toilet, so I guess she was curious about our happiness and open-minded attitude to fun. She smiled a sad smile, but she had the look of a lady who needed company. This is what Jane and I like when we can spread our love and happiness to make others happy.

The lady had a secret, but this was something of non-importance for now. She told us her name was Penny. Yes, she was not young, and maybe her hips were not perfect, but still, she had a beauty that glowed from deep within her soul. The two girls seemed to be getting drunk and were touching intimately while dancing to the music. It was getting late, and Penny had curiosity in her dark brown eyes. Our newfound friend was walking home with us, hand in hand with Jane. It seemed she wanted to delve in, encouraged by our welcoming nature. We shared an intimate and passionate night without any questions.

The following day, when I woke up, the American lady was in our bed; reality then seeped back into my consciousness. In the tangle of bed sheets, there lay Penny, a reminder of the intimacies shared under the cloak of darkness. Memories flooded back, accompanied by the dull ache of a hangover, weaving together emotions and experiences. After we said our goodbyes to Penny, our surprise companion from the grenade bar, with long hugs and wet kisses, she said, "Thanks for a memorable experience that I am sure the three of us would always treasure." Last night's therapy would ignite Penny to become more attached to life and find her happiness. We then slept until late afternoon before meeting up with a local walking tour around this lively town.

The cemeteries in this place were a great visit, and we learned about the voodoo days, arriving in the 1700s and learning the stories of the most famous voodoo queen. Marie Laveau was the original queen, and they say today that Voodoo is still alive and growing in popularity in New Orleans.

After the tour, we sought refuge in a quaint coffee shop, the aroma of freshly brewed coffee mingling with the sweet scent of beignets. As we indulged in these delectable treats, we savored each bite, savoring the unique flavors that danced upon our tongues. With bellies content and minds drifting, we allowed ourselves the luxury of simply being at that moment. We knew that life was not just about chasing grand adventures or seeking constant change. It was about finding peace within the simple moments, basking in the beauty of the present, and allowing our minds to wonder about the endless possibilities that lay before us.

As the sun set once again, casting a painting of fiery colors across the sky, we walked along the Mississippi River, our souls humming with contentment. In our ever-changing lives, we have discovered the power of embracing every twist and turn, cherishing the unexpected encounters that danced their way into our hearts. And so, as we continued our journey through the party streets of New Orleans, we knew that each day would bring new surprises, new connections, and new stories waiting to be written. For in this city that thrived on magic and a zest for life, there was no limit to the possibilities that awaited us both.

It was now the last day of our New Orleans stay, so we boarded the boat named Paddle Wheeler Creole Queen. A jazz band was onboard playing as we slowly floated down the Mississippi River. As we sailed along the majestic river, surrounded by a panorama of breathtaking scenery, we found ourselves absorbed in a sea of laughter and camaraderie. The other passengers, fueled by the festive atmosphere, shared their tales of travel and love, their words weaving a fabric of experiences that both fascinated and delighted us.

Bound by a mutual understanding, Jane and I agreed to keep our own stories hidden beneath the surface, secretly relishing in the naughty flashbacks that had unfolded between us. The scent of Penny lingered in our memories, a compelling reminder of the passion and spontaneity we had shared in the jazzy streets of New Orleans.

Four hours slipped by like a whirlwind of laughter, music, and newfound friendships, each moment cementing itself into the depths of our souls. As we bid farewell to the paddle steamer and our fellow explorers, we knew that this chapter of our journey was coming to a close.

As we gazed out at the vast expanse of the Mississippi River one final time, our eyes met, silently acknowledging the bittersweet beauty of goodbyes. With renewed determi- nation and boundless love for one another, we stepped into the unknown that awaited us on the sun-drenched shores of Miami Beach.

The next day held promises of Miami and its beaches, another destination filled with fun-loving times and sun-kissed memories waiting to be made. Though sadness lingered in our hearts at the thought of leaving behind the excitement of New Orleans, we took contentment in the knowledge that the storage of our minds would forever hold the cherished moments we had lived the dream in this city of wonders.

Chapter 16

Miami and The Caribbean.

I woke suddenly at 5 a.m. after an unusual dream that made me reminisce and gather my thoughts. I checked Jane, and she was sound asleep, looking as though she did not have a care in the world. After all, why would she? I will be looking out for her now as I would be for the rest of eternity. Our flight was early morning, so I kissed her softly on both cheeks until her eyes slowly opened. She hugged me and said, "Good morning, husband," in a calm and soft tone. Today's flight will be just a reasonably short two-hour trip.

Miami, Florida, is the place where the 1980s crime series Miami Vice, starring Don Johnson, was filmed. This was a coastal metropolis and the home where millionaires lived, and the beaches were pristine with renowned diving sites and warm sunny weather. We had four days in this city before we boarded our cruise to Cuba. Florida was the home of the beautiful Everglades National Park. The city is well known also for its strong Cuban influence.

On the first day, we walked for hours on the long stretch of iconic beaches before finding a tremendous authentic Spanish restaurant to take away our hunger, and corona beers quenched our thirst. The following day, at 6 a.m., we were shaken by the loud, piercing buzz of the hotel phone. Half asleep, I thought I was having a nightmare when the voice on the other end of the phone answered, "Good morning, this is Patricia Allen from the Royal Caribbean." This was the company we were booked to travel with for our Cuban cruise.

The voice was very apologetic and announced the unsettling news that our cruise itinerary had changed. Her given reason was that the US government had now restricted cruise boats entering Cuba from the United States. Devastation touched my insides as Cuba was one place I was thrilled about and dreaming of visiting. As disappointed as we were, we accepted a fifty percent discount on the cruise fare and the new itinerary. Now, it seemed we would spend a week cruising around the Caribbean Islands. The catastrophic announcement stopped me and Jane from sleeping any further so I made us both a very strong hot coffee to discuss our decision thoroughly. It was then we both agreed to go with the new itinerary. We also promised each other we would see Cuba another time in the future.

Life has its twists and turns, and disappointment is part of the journey, and we know this. We were very optimistic that the Caribbean Islands still had memories to offer us, and after all, the important thing that mattered was that we would visit new destinations together.

Late afternoon, we went to visit Calle Ocho, which was known as Little Havana. This place was at least a window to the culture of the country whose famous identities were Fidel Castro Ruz, leader of the Cuban revolution, and Carlos Manuel de Cespedes y Del Castillo, Father of the Homeland. Little Havana was full of bright-colored buildings, art galleries, and cafes that sold Cuban coffee and, of course, Cuban cigars.

Early evening, the rhythmic bands started to play with Latin music filling the air, and the bars were beginning to fill up with people from all walks of life. Enticed by the alluring sounds and smells emanating from the lively bars and cafés, we found ourselves lost in the sea of people, mingling with locals and tourists alike, captivated by the contagious joy and warmth that surrounded us. As we sat sipping mojitos, watching the salsa dancers move to the beat of the drums, we realized that although we may never be able to visit Cuba physically, we had already experienced a small piece of its magic. We celebrated the spirit of the Cuban people, their passion for life, their love of music and dance, and their unrelenting spirit.

We kissed before sleeping, and Jane asked if we were in Cuba today. I answered with deep thinking, "Maybe we were, as the Cuban people we saw were trying to give the illusion that Little Havana was Cuba and not Miami." We carried with us the memories of Little Havana, the taste of Cuban coffee, and the rhythm of Latin music, knowing that these experiences would stay with us forever. And who knows, maybe one day we will find ourselves in Cuba, living out our Cuban dream.

Time passed, and it was now time to leave Miami with the ship's horn signaling our departure aboard "Empress of the Sea" for our cruise through the Bahamas. We were not disappointed with our room onboard, our home for the next seven days. We left Miami with a newfound appreciation for the power of illusion and the potency of cultural exchange. We were on the top deck sipping red wine and looking at each other, wondering about the new destinations we would visit in the days ahead. The reality was that we were both in love with each other's company, as it continually seemed our romance story was written before we arrived on Earth.

After our first day on our luxury cruise boat that was spent at sea, we took advantage of this rest day, and with the slow rocking of our boat on the calm waters, we caught up on much-needed sleep. On the second day, we docked at the beautiful Grand Caymans with white sand and warm waters. This day was enjoyed at the beach, and we maybe overdid the sunshine as we were a bit sunburned at day's end, but worth it all to visit this magical town of beaches. We held hands, and we were living life as a married couple on a dream honeymoon. Our love, once strong, had become even stronger.

The following day, the ship stopped at Belize and Costa Maya, Mexico, where we ventured around these new places, looking to see what was to see in these sleepy little towns that the modern world had forgotten.

The final stop was Key West, Florida, the highlight of the cruise. This island city is the southernmost point of the United States, lying just ninety miles North of Cuba. The day we arrived was the annual pride fiesta with a nude parade feature down Duval Street, the main drag in the downtown area.

Embracing the spirit of the event, we joined in the festivities, shedding our inhibitions along with our clothes. Our bodies became canvases, splattered with paint, transforming us into living pieces of art. As we paraded through the streets, laughter filled the air, and we felt an overwhelming sense of belonging. Strangers became friends, bonded by a shared appreciation for individuality and the freedom to express themselves without judgment.

As the sun began to set, we reluctantly made our way back to the ship. But the memories we made in Key West will forever be in our hearts. Key West had shown us that life is meant to be celebrated and that love knows no bounds. We were grateful for the opportunity to experience such a unique and inspiring event. We knew that our journey together was far from over and that the most incredible surprises were still awaiting us.

Chapter 17

Canada and Seattle.

Our hotel in Toronto was located at the bottom end of the risqué Yonge Street, the red-light district of the city. The first morning, we were on a bus heading up to Niagara Falls, and after the two-hour smooth ride gazing out the bus window at the scenery, we arrived.

My love grew strong at this wonder of the world that gave the energy that projected feelings of love. It's no wonder that this natural wonder has been dubbed the Honeymoon Capital of the World, for everywhere we looked, romance was in the air. Even Jerome Bonaparte, brother of Napoleon, chose this setting for his honeymoon. Here at the famous falls, Marilyn Monroe stayed and confessed it was one of her favorite places in the world. Imagine the thunderous roar of the water as it plummeted down, creating a breathtaking cascade of white-tipped waves. Jane and I were astonished to be now looking at the tons of rushing water over the Falls that flowed from the great lakes to this final destination.

As we basked in the glory of Niagara Falls, something changed within us. The lush greenery that surrounded us added to the magical feeling, and we felt as if we had been transported to a different world. The energy of the water and the power it possessed filled us with a sense of awe and reverence, and our love for each other blossomed. The capability of nature is immense and can awaken emotions within us that we never knew we had. Niagara Falls may be a natural wonder, but it has the ability to create wonders in our hearts as well.

Jane and I found a restaurant with a view that looked directly over the falls, giving the feel we were about to flow over the edge. It was now sunset, which was one time of the day Jane and I always enjoyed. We drank some red wine and ate well in this perfect spot with the spray of water from below, giving the lowering sun a perspective of calmness that maybe only this time of day always permitted us to feel. I am not sure if it was the wine or the feeling that the falls gave me as, looking into her eyes, sounding as corny as I could, I told Jane "My love for you was bigger and stronger than Niagara Falls itself, and it flowed longer and deeper." Jane smiled, curious and maybe a bit embarrassed how corny I became, she looked into my eyes, and whispered with a kiss, "I love you".

The last bus that was heading back to Toronto was 10 p.m., so after twelve hours at this incredible waterfall, we were on that last bus and heading home to our Yonge Street hotel. The energy and calmness these wondrous falls gave could not be explained in words, but only a visit here would answer the mystery feeling.

On the second day of our trip, we boarded the hop-on-hop-off bus to explore the many attractions that Toronto had to offer. The first stop was the iconic CN Tower, once the tallest building in the world, towering at a staggering height of five hundred and thirty-three meters. The next stop was the enchanting Casa Loma castle. The magnificent structure, with its gothic architecture and sprawling gardens. Stopping at various other landmarks, each one more inspiring than the last. With the sun setting on the horizon, we bid farewell to the bustling city and headed back to the comfort of our hotel.

Toronto was a friendly city, and very open-minded people inhabited the city. With this in mind, we both thought, and I said to Jane, "Let's go see what we can discover." We wandered up Yonge Street, which had the reputation as the naughty street at night, having a few beers at a bar full of friendly people. As we drank our beers, little did we know that this night would take an unforeseen turn. To our surprise, we were joined by a couple who introduced themselves as Tim and Patricia. It was then that the couple, with an air of openness and boldness, extended an invitation to an exclusive club. Jane looked at me, and I looked at her, and we said, "Sure! Why not?".

This was our first time to go to one of these clubs, and even though we had a little apprehension, it opened our eyes to a world of sexual freedom. We sat at the bar inside the club, and my new friend's wife started kissing Jane passionately. And Tim and I just smiled with approval. Within the walls of this liberating space, secrets were shared. Tim confided to us, revealing his attraction to both men and women. Encouraged by the atmosphere of acceptance, Tim set forth on his journey of self-discovery, leaving us to enjoy the company of his wife, Patricia. The passion ignited, fueled by the flames of consent and mutual desire.

In the quiet sanctuary of a private room, the sounds of moans mingled with sighs of ecstasy as bodies merged and pleasure blossomed. Time slipped away, lost in the realm of pure sensation, until the agreed-upon rendezvous hour approached. The liberating energy of sexual exploration in the depths of Toronto's nights, our exploits with the open-mindedness that thrived within the city, unearthing desires we never knew existed, and forging connections that would forever mark our journey through life.

Arriving back at our agreed meeting spot, Tim was already waiting with another man. They then kissed and said goodbye. I was a little surprised, but of course, there was no judgment from me, and we all left this unique, eye-opening club together. We thanked Tim and Patricia for their friendship and for showing us a club that was unique in every way possible. Patricia taught us a thing or two about lovemaking, and another memory was now in our minds forever. We had one last day in Toronto to get fit, try out the hotel spa, and enjoy a blissful, relaxing therapeutic massage.

We loved Toronto, but tomorrow, our next stop was Vancouver in British Columbia, named after Captain George Vancouver in the late 1700s. We flew with Air Canada, and it was a long five-hour flight. Because of the time difference, we arrived late at night.

Our days were always busy, but we liked to keep moving, finding escapades, exploring, and searching out new happenings in new places. As we woke up the following day, Jane and I were excited to start our exploration of Vancouver. This picturesque city was wet and rainy. Jane and I continued to seek out new experiences, from trying new foods at local restaurants to taking a bike ride through Stanley Park. As we reflected on our travels so far, we realized that the most crucial part of any journey is not the destination but the stories we gather along the way.

Indeed, it was nice to be crazy and explore naughty things sometimes, but being alone with Jane was my true contentment. We would leave Canada tomorrow morning on an early Amtrak train trip to Seattle, a three-hour picturesque trip along the Cascades route with the beauty of the scenery that mesmerized us both before arriving relaxed in all ways possible.

In Seattle, we arrived with time to visit the Fremont Markets and Pike Place Fish Markets, serving up fresh, delicious Alaskan Salmon. Our day was not complete until we found the original Starbucks nearby Pike Street Markets that opened in 1971, and after an hour's wait in line, we sampled their coffee even though it was nighttime. We slept like babies as soon as the coffee wore off, ready for another day in Seattle.

We visited the Seattle Space Needle, a six-hundred-and-five-foot-tall observation tower at the center of Seattle. Then, our afternoon was spent on board the Duck Tour by land and water on a World War II amphibious landing craft, learning in a humorous way from the comedian driver and guide explaining the stories of the rainy city. We traveled all over the city, and on the water part of the tour, we passed by the houseboat used for filming the 1993 movie Sleepless in Seattle.

By nightfall, Jane and I talked about our honeymoon, especially the fantastic sights of the US and Canada. Tomorrow, we had a flight to London with British Airways direct to Heathrow Airport. We would spend over a month more traveling in the United Kingdom and Europe on our honeymoon, which seemed never-ending. Jane was my angel, and with her beside me, excitement was all that was in my mind as we boarded our nine-hour direct flight.

Chapter 18

London England.

Our flight onboard the Airbus 380 was an experience. This aircraft was the largest and heaviest aircraft ever built. Inside, the cabin was spacious and comfortable, making our long journey to the United Kingdom more bearable. Landing was perfect, with no bumping and no friction from the outside weather. We made our way through immigration, and a sense of unease crept over me. The immigration officer's intense questioning caught me off guard. He delved into personal details, asking questions that seemed unnecessary and intrusive. My confusion grew as this questioning began to resemble more of an interrogation than a routine check.

Although I felt a surge of frustration building inside me, I knew better than to lose my composure. I smiled politely, keeping my lips sealed, aware that any outburst or expression of disagreement could jeopardize our entry into the country. It was a battle between my emotions and rationale, a test of self-control. It perplexed me why such intense questioning was necessary. We were merely two travelers seeking to explore and experience the wonders of the United Kingdom. I understood that immigration officers have to ensure the safety and security of their borders, still, it felt excessive and unwarranted.

Eventually, after what seemed like an eternity, we were granted entry and released from the grip of interrogation. An old quote says, "When a man is tired of London, he is tired of life, for there is in London all that life can afford," so it seems Jane and I will find plenty to do in the city of Brolley.

We stayed across the road from The Big Ben, located at Westminster Abbey, with views of the Thames River ready to circulate the city. The first morning, we were onboard the original red open-air bus touring the city wearing warm jackets that were water resistant. This was a good move as it was cold, with a fine drizzle slowly falling from the grey sky above. The weather was no match for our spirits. As we sat on the top deck of the bus, the cool mist brushed against our cheeks, a gentle reminder that we were in one of the most iconic cities in the world. It would take a lot more than the natural elements to bother the naughty married couple.

The sights unfolded before us, each landmark steeped in architecture and grandeur. From the regal Buckingham Palace to the majestic Tower Bridge, the city revealed its secrets with every passing mile. Our excitement grew, matched only by our resilience against the weather. As the bus glided through the bustling streets of London, we couldn't help but marvel at the energy and diversity that surrounded us. The rain, though persistent, was a minor inconvenience. It did nothing to dampen our spirits or our determination to immerse ourselves in the lively atmosphere of this magnificent city.

London was indeed a city that never slept, never tired. And neither would we, for there was in London all that life could afford, and we were ready to embrace it with open hearts and adventurous spirits. We captured sweet, memorable photos all day at our numerous stops and, at nightfall, ended up in an Irish pub at the center of Piccadilly Circus. Here, we relaxed and sampled some pints of Guinness, listening to the Irish band playing folk songs from times gone by, and ended up arriving home late but buzzing from a day that dreams are made of.

Earlier at the bar, the locals were being smart ass and calling us Romeo and Juliet, but we did not care. I guess the reason was we continually held each other and sweetly kissed little kisses from time to time. I took it as a compliment and was not offended. Londoners were known as being jokers and were only having fun with their lover's jokes aimed at us. Besides, I was quick myself and had respectful comebacks to their humor. I even said to them, "My family name is Shakespeare." They looked at me with confusion; maybe they almost believed me.

We stayed at our hotel the next day, with just a morning walk across the bridge to take a better look at Westminster Abbey and the Tower of Big Ben, the city's most famous clock. This Church of England is the setting for most Royal marriages and, of course, Royal funerals. As the afternoon approached, we hopped on the Tube to make our way to the bustling hub of Piccadilly Circus. The spirited energy of the city was palpable as we made our way through the crowds of people. We were fortunate enough to snag two tickets with seats close to the stage for the night's West End production of Mama Mia.

There was an undeniable aura of excitement in the air as we settled into our seats and waited for the curtain to rise. This would make a perfect end to an unforgettable day. The show was scheduled to start at 8 p.m., but we were already there at the Novello Theatre by 7 p.m. We watched the love story of a girl named Sophie trying to find out who was her real dad with a choice of three. The music was perfect with all the songs from the 70s group Abba.

The finale of the show had the whole audience get out of their seats and sing and dance to the music of "Waterloo," "Mama Mia," and Dancing Queen." This was a show that you would watch many times and never get tired of this performance. Another memorable night with my destiny wife Jane, whom I loved more than words.

We relaxed on our final day in London with vivid memories of Mama Mia still in our minds. Night time found me and Jane out in the red-light district of Soho. Bars catering to gay and straight, sex shops, and the ladies of the night were the regular attractions happening at Soho. We found ourselves getting excited by the feel of Soho, and soon, we noticed a gay and lesbian bar that had excellent dance music being performed by a band wearing bright rainbow-colored outfits.

As we entered the bar, we noticed many eyes were looking at us. I guess the boys were looking at me and the girls at Jane. I was not concerned as we were discreetly acting like friends before ordering two pints of beer served with a smile by the overacting gay barman. Accordingly, we said a warm thanks and also sent him back a warm smile. We sat alone, and no one bothered us, just a few smiles and hellos from others. We watched what was going on in this bar with a difference, and the dance floor was full of a free, happy crowd. This free crowd did not care who or what they were, as they just acted naturally. I admired these people; they were not interested in acting fake, just being themselves, whatever their sexual persuasion they preferred.

Two middle-aged ladies were looking closely at me and Jane before asking to join our table, and coincidently, we had two extra seats to accommodate them. These ladies were a friendly couple and were born in this stunning city, and we appreciated their company, telling us many stories of London town. Our new companions asked no questions, and we did the same. Just talking, drinking, and laughing, and before long, the three girls were dancing and having a great time. I sat alone, getting smiles from different men, but luckily, none of them approached me.

Before long, all four of us were in a black London taxi as our new friends insisted on seeing us safely back to our hotel. They also insisted on buying us an excellent breakfast the following day to talk more. At 8 a.m., we were treated to breakfast at a fancy restaurant on the Thames River. Then, after eating and drinking some of the best coffee I have ever tasted, it was time to say goodbye, and then, with some kisses and hugs, we parted ways. We had a 2 p.m. flight to Cannes, France, so by the time we packed, we were soon checked out and heading to Gatwick Airport for a two-hour flight to the French Riviera town.

Chapter 19

Paris and Cannes, France.

Once at Cannes Airport, we hired a car that would take us to our hotel in town. Our driver was a young man with a deep French accent and a friendly demeanor. He told us stories about Cannes as we drove towards the town that celebrates the Palais des Festivals, the Cannes Film Festival that is held every year.

It was about a forty-minute drive from the airport, and the winding road looped around the picturesque headland, giving a view of beauty that only nature can provide. In the distance, many sailing yachts and power-driven cruisers could be seen in the clear, calm ocean waters. I could only imagine what was happening on those lavish boats and started dreaming that I was onboard, also joining their parties fueled by French champagne.

The French Riviera attracts visitors from around the world for its climate, beaches, and medieval villages. It is well known for its luxury appeal and is the playground of the rich and famous French and European millionaires. On our first morning, we strolled along the beach hand in hand with the blue sky above as clear as could be imagined possible. Almost to the point that maybe one or more of the renowned French artists in heaven were splashing deep blue colors to make the sky even bluer than blue. Before long, we found an old-fashioned café with the aroma of the coffee too strong to walk past. While sitting looking into my wife's eyes, Jane was sending me warmth that I felt inside my body.

Cannes was sunny but cold as it was nearing Christmas, with a temperature of maybe three degrees. It did not worry us; we were wearing matching thick jackets that we bought from Savile Row when we were in London. Here we sat, admiring boats and yachts of all descriptions moored on the bay, and they all looked expensive with some total luxury and elegance.

As we moved along with our day, we found an old-fashioned movie theatre and watched the movie version of Jersey Boys adapted from the stage musical that we watched in Singapore. Excited for the next chapter of our endless honeymoon, tomorrow we will be on board the train to Paris for five days to celebrate Christmas in the "City of Love."

After a long five-hour train trip, we arrived mid-afternoon at Gare de Norde, the busiest railway station in Europe. We hailed a taxi, and soon, we arrived at our destination, Champs Elysees. This connects the Arc de Triomphe with the Place de la Concorde and is considered to be one of the world's most iconic streets. We checked into the Marriott Hotel. Luckily, I had enough reward points for our stay, as hotels in this area were costly. This street was a flurry of activity, with locals and tourists alike hurrying to their destinations.

In the midst of the biting cold, wrapped in layers upon layers of warmth, we ventured out into the early morning darkness. Our destination, the must-see Eiffel Tower, stands tall as a testament to human ingenuity and archi-tectural marvel. Freezing waiting in line for almost two hours, it was now our turn to ascend to the top of the tower named after the engineer Gustave Eiffel, whose company built this wrought iron lattice tower from 1887 to 1889 originally as the centerpiece of the 1889 World Fair. After what felt like an eternity, with frozen fingers and frost-kissed cheeks, we ascended the tower's intricate lattice, each step filling us with awe and wonder. The panoramic views of Paris greeted us from every angle as if the city itself had dressed up in a dazzling array of lights and colors just for our arrival.

From the top, we could see the sprawling boulevards and grand architecture, the Seine River winding its way through the heart of the city. With wide eyes, we pointed out acclaimed landmarks: the Louvre, Notre Dame, and the Champs-Élysées, each holding its own story and secrets. The world seemed to shrink, and we realized that despite our differences, we were all connected by the shared wonder and beauty of this breathtaking view.

Like a miracle or a sign from above, light snow began to fall, and Jane and I kissed at the top of the world or at least this magical tower. I spoke in a French voice, "Je vous aime," which in English is "I love you," and when I said it, tears of happiness dampened Jane's eyes, and her happiness lit up the city of love. The light snowfall was a new experience, feeling the damp, cold Paris air gently freezing our noses and faces.

As we descended from the tower, our hearts were ablaze with a renewed sense of adventure. The cold had transformed me from an adversary to a companion on this remarkable journey. As we left the Eiffel Tower behind, its silhouette fading into the distance, we carried the memories of that freezing morning with us. For within the depths of winter, we had found warmth and a belief that anything is possible when we dare to dream and drift with the world, even in the harshest of conditions.

The next day, we visited the Louvre Museum. As we stepped foot into a world of wonder before our eyes, we were humbled by the sheer size of the collection on display. From Ancient Greek sculptures to Renaissance masterpieces, the Louvre was a treasure trove of art and history. The marble statues whispered tales of Gods and Goddesses, frozen in time but alive with emotion. Their elegant forms seemed to reach out to us, inviting us to understand the beauty and complexity of the ancient world.

Moving through the halls of the museum, we marveled at the Renaissance paintings that had captured the essence of human emotions for centuries and brought forth a sense of wonder. The brushstrokes of Da Vinci, the vivid colors of Van Gogh, and the enigmatic smiles of the Mona Lisa made our imaginations send us to different eras. The scene depicted a woman lost in thought, her expression a delicate balance of sorrow and hope. It was a moment frozen in time, a glimpse into the artist's vulnerabilities. As we stood before the distinctive painting of the Mona Lisa to catch a glimpse of the enigmatic subject, we felt a sense of humility and reverence. Mona Lisa, painted by Leonardo da Vinci, has hung proudly on display here at the Louvre since 1797.

As we stepped back into the bustling streets of Paris, we carried a new perspective with us. We understood that art has the power to transcend time, to bridge cultures, and to evoke universal emotions. The Louvre Museum has gifted us with a glimpse into the infinite possibilities of human creativity and the enduring legacy of our shared humanity. At this moment, we realized that Paris truly lived up to its reputation as the City of Love and Light. It was a city that captured our hearts and left us with memories that would last a lifetime.

As we exited the place, we thought we would walk back to Champs Elysees. We enjoyed the cold feel of the air as we walked briskly to keep our bodies warm. The snow had abated, so we postponed our walk and sat outside a quaint sidewalk café lured by the smell of the fresh, warm croissants and hot, aromatic coffee. While at the café, sipping on our steaming cups of coffee and indulging in the buttery goodness of the freshly baked croissants, we couldn't help but feel a sense of contentment wash over us. The hustle and bustle of the city seemed to fade away, replaced by the cozy atmosphere of the café and the comforting aroma that surrounded us.

Christmas was nearing, but we still had two days of seeing the Paris sights, so here we are at Notre-Dame de Paris, meaning "Our Lady of Paris." This Catholic Cathedral, dedicated to the Virgin Mary, was a fine example of French Gothic architecture. We lit a candle for our departed and said prayers, and being at this church, we felt they were beside us in the mystic spirit world.

From a solemn mood to a party mood with our night at Moulin Rouge. We were captivated by the entertainment of the long-legged sexy girls dancing the Can Can to the lively beat, which was a very high-energy, physically demanding dance, and we dipped in the cheerful atmosphere of the night and went back to our hotel.

On our next day was a visit to Montmartre, the bohemian neighborhood perched high above the city. We braved the steep climb up to the top of the hill, rewarded with sweeping views of Paris below. The iconic white dome of Sacré-Coeur Basilica stood tall against the winter sky, its hallowed halls echoing with the murmurs of prayer. We stood on the steps of the church, watching as the city twinkled in the distance, the lights like stars in the night sky. The sight was like a painting coming to life, each brushstroke adding depth and texture to the canvas.

It was one day before Christmas, so we seized our chance for a trip up the Reine River by boat. As we sailed down the Reine River, the chilly Paris air bit our hands and fingers. But we were mesmerized by the beauty of the riverbanks, with each turn revealing a new vista more breathtaking than the last. We saw old stone bridges arching over the waters and Grand Gothic structures towering over the river. It was like being in a dream - a winter wonderland straight out of a fairytale.

Christmas day was now upon us, with the white snow returning for us with an unexpected gift, nature's way of bestowing upon us a true White Christmas. Today was a day of gift-giving to my sweet wife, and her gift to me was her presence beside me. I loved the smell and the taste of Jane, who never left my side all day as we roamed the streets and boulevards by foot on the snow-covered pavements of this city built from the visionary of centuries of the past with its historical buildings for all walks of life to see.

We ventured for hours, our footprints leaving imprints on the untouched snow. The world seemed different, transformed into a serene and magical place. We didn't need grand gestures or extravagant gifts; all we needed was the love and connection we felt in each other's arms. We just surrendered to the power of love and the beauty of simplicity. In that instant, the materialistic nature of gifts faded away, and the true meaning of Christmas shone through.

Chapter 20

Amsterdam and Barcelona.

The morning was upon us as we continued our journey. We boarded the Thalys high-speed train to Amsterdam. We carried every memory with us, ready for the next leg of our journey, excited for the surprises and joys that lay ahead. I drifted into a peaceful sleep as the rhythmic motion of the train lulled me into a dreamlike state. A three hour and twenty minutes train trip to our destination that was spent sleeping in my angel's arms. It was a serene beginning to our quest in the capital of the Netherlands.

As we arrived at the station, Amsterdam welcomed us with open arms, ready to display its rich cultural heritage. The city was known worldwide for its artistic heritage, elaborate canal system, and gabled facades, legacies of the 17th-century Golden Age. We hired two pushbikes to tour this city of bicycles and canals. Our first stop was the Anne Frank House, a place that held the weight of history within its walls. As we walked through the hidden rooms, our hearts filled with the knowledge of the young Jewish girl who lived in fear during the dark times of the Nazi occupation. Her story served as a stark reminder of the resilience of the human spirit.

Next, Vincent van Gogh at his eponymous museum. This passionate artist cut off his ear in a fit of rage and eventually took his own life and died penniless. His distinctive masterpieces spoke volumes about his passion and inner turmoil. Standing in front of his famous self-portraits, I couldn't help but feel a profound sadness for an artist whose brilliance went unrecognized in his lifetime. To lighten the mood, we headed to the Heineken Experience, a temple dedicated to the art of brewing. We delved into the legendary beer's origination, taking a step back in time to understand the craftsmanship that goes into every bottle, with the beer tasting being the perfect finale.

As the day came to a close, we continued to cycle along the picturesque canals, the fading sunlight casting a golden glow over the gabled facades. Amsterdam had reminded us of the beauty that can be found in both the brightest and darkest corners of the city. With hearts full of gratitude and minds brimming with newfound knowledge, we returned our bicycles, cherishing the times we spent in this city. Amsterdam had opened our eyes to the power of art, resilience, and the simple joy of cycling through life's winding paths.

It was a Friday night, and people were out and about. We arrived at Dam Square, The Red-Light District. Marijuana smoke filled the air along with music from the nightclubs, with some bands playing live music, and some clubs had DJs. Jane and I talked to people, both locals and visitors from all parts of the world, sharing some of our travel stories and listening to their stories.

Walking back to our hotel, we were surprised by the ladies of the night or, to be blunt, prostitutes. These ladies stood or were sitting in the front of their brothel with opened windows for all to see what they were offering, and they were not hiding anything. Sex workers were legal here in this open-minded city, but no photos were allowed. We stopped to chat with a tall, blonde, gorgeous lady who seemed very friendly, but of course, they had to be as this was their living. Whether it was the marijuana smoke or the Heineken beers, I asked, "How much for an hour?". Jane was surprised at my question, and I think maybe this lady had seen it all and would have entertained the kinkiest sex acts.

Then she said to come in for an hour and offered a reasonably cheap price. As we went inside, the people on the streets were observing us entering her room as she closed the curtains. I kissed this Lady Godiva lookalike passionately, and then we both kissed Jane. Before long, we were all undressed and let our desires take over our inhibitions, and wow!, what an hour of absolute passion we had. We then kissed this lady bye-bye and waved bye-bye again as we walked out of her sight. Jane then looked into my eyes and said, "You are so naughty!". I grinned and then squeezed her hand tightly as we walked home, feeling a good night was experienced by the honeymooners.

We had one more day in this city of open-minded people and just spent most of our last day at the hotel eating well and resting from our tiring days. We took a canal cruise before sunset to complete our Amsterdam tour, learning more stories of this ageless city. The canal cruise was worth it and showed the city from a different and unique perspective. Tomorrow, we have a flight to Barcelona, Spain.

After the two-hour flight from Amsterdam Schiphol Airport to Barcelona-El Prat Airport, we arrived at our hotel just two days before New Year's and we were organized and ready to explore at daybreak. The first day, we went out early. It was cold, but there was no snow in Barcelona as here snow is a very rare event. Our first stop was the Sagrada Familia, the most iconic architectural masterpiece designed by Antoni Gaudi, who had his footprint all over this city.

It is the largest unfinished Catholic Church in the world. Inside this one-of-a-kind church, it took our breath away. The unique workmanship was something you could not imagine possible until you entered. The Basilica's use of color, space, and stonework was just jaw-dropping. Jane and I looked at each other with amazed eyes, and both agreed it was worth visiting Barcelona just to see this church. We spent all day seeing the sights of this historic city that was the starting point of the Italian explorer Christopher Columbus on his voyage, where he discovered the New World of the Americas on board his ship, Santa Maria.

It was now the 31st of December, the eve of the New Year. Jane and I stumbled upon a hidden gem in Barcelona - an old-fashioned bar radiating with the brilliant sounds of Spanish folk music. Flamenco guitarists strummed their strings with fiery passion while a female vocalist serenaded the crowd with her perfect voice, weaving tales of love and longing. Caught up in the enchanting atmosphere, Jane and I surrendered to the rhythm of the music, dancing with the locals and enjoying ourselves in the lively celebration. The energy was infectious, and we quickly made friends with the spirited crowd, sharing stories and creating memories that would last a lifetime.

As midnight approached, we were each handed twelve grapes, a cherished Spanish tradition symbolizing luck for the twelve months ahead. We joined in the festive countdown, savoring the sweet taste of each grape as the final seconds of the year slipped away. Glasses of sparkling champagne were raised in unison, toasting a future filled with joy and prosperity. Following the local customs,

Jane and I placed money in our shoes and pockets and clenched it in our hands, hoping to attract good fortune in the coming year. With anticipation building, the clock struck midnight, and I couldn't help but steal kisses from Jane and the Spanish senoritas who eagerly took pleasure in the tradition. Exhaustion mingled with exhilaration. In the privacy of our room, I gave Jane my wettest, sweetest, and longest kiss of the night, sealing our love and excitement for tomorrow's flight to Rome.

Chapter 21

Rome and Berlin.

After a two-hour flight from Barcelona, we landed at Fiumicino Leonardo da Vinci Airport, named after the legendary Italian Inventor, who is also known for his paintings of the Mona Lisa and the Last Supper. Then, a taxi ride from the airport, and we were now at the city that was full of chronicles dating back to the days of the legendary Roman Emperors. We found ourselves trenched in the heart of Rome, where ancient ruins and captivating stories awaited.

Eager to explore the sights, Jane and I strolled towards the Trevi Fountain, a majestic masterpiece steeped in legend. The sound of rushing water grew louder as we approached, and our anticipation mounted. I could feel the magic in the air, as if the very essence of Rome was captured within the splashing waters. With a glimmer of excitement in her eyes, Jane turned to me. It was as though she knew my wish before I even spoke it. At that moment, our connection deepened, and I felt that our hearts beat in sync, yearning for a lifetime of togetherness.

I reached into my pocket, retrieved a coin, and held it tightly in my hand. With a smile, I looked into Jane's eyes. Then together, we raised our hands and released the coin into the fountain, our wishes mingling with the countless others cast before us. In that tender moment, I

133

pulled Jane close, savoring the warmth of her embrace. Our lips met in a loving kiss, each touch conveying a promise of forever. It was a kiss filled with tenderness, passion, and the unspoken vow to always be there for one another through every joy and challenge that life would bring. We continued our exploration of this ancient city, ready to uncover the secrets and stories that whispered from every cobblestone and monument. Rome gave us a feeling of belonging, and we were prepared to appreciate all that it had to offer, knowing that our love would guide us on this extraordinary journey.

The hard work of making wishes made us hungry, and it seemed all restaurants served the same menu. We chose a restaurant that had softly playing Italian Opera music in the background. We had no idea what the words to the songs were, but it was sung theatrically. We ordered pizza and pasta and a bottle of Italian red wine as this was all that was on the menu, so "When in Rome, eat like the Romans." We ate until our hearts were content, and wow! We were overfull, so we wandered the streets of Rome until midnight.

The architecture of the city was a classic style of the past centuries. Walking these streets of this ancient city was like a museum displaying statues and buildings from a past time still standing to be admired by one and all. Rome was a city of antiquity dating back centuries, so the next day, we went inside the Sistine Chapel with the works of Michelangelo painted in magnificent High Renaissance Art on the ceiling of the Cathedral painted in perfection between 1508 and 1512 with patience and skill unique only to this talented artist.

Leaving the chapel, we made our way to the grandeur of Vatican City. It stood as a testament to centuries of devotion, an embodiment of spirituality and artistic brilliance. The sheer size and magnitude of the structures left us stunned, while the knowledge that this was the very heart of the Roman Catholic Church imbued it with a sense of profound significance. This truly remarkable structure is the most sacred place in Christianity and attests to an undeniable faith and a formidable spiritual venture.

As we bid farewell to this sacred place, we carried with us not only memories of magnificent architecture and sublime art but also a deep appreciation for the immeasurable impact that Rome and its spiritual center had on the course of human history.

We saved the best until last, the Coliseum, where, in ancient times, the Gladiators would fight until the death. This barbaric ritual would entertain huge crowds and the Emperors of Rome. It was built two thousand years ago during the reign of the Flavian emperors as a gift to the Roman people. They say over four hundred thousand gladi-ators were killed here while the crowds cheered for blood. The "sport" was appallingly brutal, and many gladiators faced the arena with fear and trembling. Some were even forced to square off against wild animals. There was an occasion written in chronicles where twenty gladiators committed group suicide rather than enter the arena. The lucky ones managed to win their freedom by winning many battles. Jane and I felt the pain of these brave warriors as we spent most of our day in this giant Amphitheatre.

As we left the ancient walls behind, a mix of emotions swirled within us - sadness, anger, and a renewed apprecia-tion for the sanctity of life. The Coliseum had left an indel-ible mark upon our souls, reminding us of the importance of empathy and compassion in a world that can so easily succumb to its darker impulses. I could see the sadness on my angel's face as she found it hard to comprehend that humans could be so cruel to each other. It was often claimed that Christians were persecuted for their refusal to worship the emperor, and some were supposedly even fed to the lions as entertainment.

After a sobering day at the Coliseum, we spent our last night in front of the hotel fire to keep us warm, sipping on some Italian prosecco. This night was romantic, and our lives were full of closeness built on love. Jane hugged me close to her naked body all night; I guess she was feeling disturbed by the Gladiator stories we heard. Tomorrow, we would fly to Berlin for a short stay and see more of what life's past events could show us in this German capital city.

Landing in Berlin, Germany, after a smooth two-hour flight onboard a Boeing 737, we learned from the conversation with the flight attendants, as they gave us a little knowledge of our new town. We boarded a boat and glided along the calm waters. We were served Kolsch, a traditional German beer, in large glasses. The amber liquid danced with effervescence, reflecting the festive atmosphere that surrounded us. We joined in the chorus of voices, laughter mingling with song, as the other passengers embraced the joyous spirit of the moment.

The Germans, known for their robust physiques and hearty spirits, indulged in the art of seasoned drinking. They effortlessly consumed three beers to our one, embodying an age-old tradition that tied their culture together. In their revelry, they taught us to savor the simple pleasures of life, to raise our glasses high, and to let our voices soar. The Second World War had torn this place apart, separating the East from the West. But now, standing on the deck of the boat, we saw a city that had risen above the ashes, a testament to the resilience and the unyielding human spirit.

The next day, we were at the most infamous place in the city called Checkpoint Charlie. It was called and was the crossing point of the Berlin Wall, which divided East and

West Germany with the Soviet Communist rule in the East and freedom in the West, where over one hundred and forty people died trying to cross to the West from 1961 until its collapse in 1989.

Jane and I uncovered the authentic stories of Berlin, especially on the East side, which was still a place known for its past communist rule. It was the 9th of November 1989, five days after half a million people gathered in East Berlin in a mass protest, until the pivotal moment in time when the wall was pulled down and the country was again unified into one.

Our trip to Berlin was mostly sightseeing, and the remarkable sights of this city were one of a divided era dating back in time. It was now time to leave Berlin and the next stop was only a quick one-hour flight away to Copenhagen Castrup Airport.

Chapter 22

Copenhagen, Norway, Sweden, The Baltic Cruise.

Copenhagen is a relaxed capital city of Denmark. As dusk settled over the city, we found ourselves in the heart of it all - the city center with a corona beer in hand and the aroma of Danish hotdogs filling the air. At this moment, we felt a profound sense of contentment. The city made us feel welcome, inviting us to bask in its laid-back charm and soak up the unique Danish spirit.

Surrounded by the cheerful atmosphere, we watched as street performers scattered throughout the square captivating the passersby. The sound of music filled the air, drawing us closer to a talented busker strumming his acoustic guitar. His soulful voice, combined with the strings, created a perfect harmony that resonated within us. It felt like having a front-row seat at an intimate concert, the melodies weaving through the night. Time was moving slowly as we became lost in the beauty of the music, each note stirring something deep within our hearts.

The next day, we ventured to the waterfront where the Little Mermaid Statue resided. Perched delicately on the edge of the water, she gazed longingly towards the horizon. A symbol of Hans Christian Andersen's timeless tale, she reminded us of the power of dreams and the allure of the unknown.

As we explored further, we discovered the prosperous fortunes and royal traditions of Denmark. In the heart of the city, a regal presence lingered - the King of Denmark still held court, carrying on the country's storied past. We spent romantic days walking on the water's edge, and most nights became a routine of listening to buskers perform for the crowds. We left Denmark at night time, taking the overnight boat to Oslo, Norway, a nineteen-hour trip on calm and smooth waters. We waved goodbye to Copenhagen as tomorrow morning, Oslo would be our boat's arrival point. The gentle hum of the boat's engines lulled us into a state of tranquility as we strolled along the top deck. The cool breeze caressed our faces, carrying with it the scent of the open sea. The moon and stars danced above us, their twinkling light guiding our journey into the unknown. Jane and I romanced on the top deck and went to our cabin early and made love with the gentle rocking of the boat and then slept a long, deep sleep in our cozy, comfortable bed.

As the sun broke through the horizon, its gentle rays piercing through the curtains of our cabin, we were awakened by the resounding horn that marked our arrival in Norway. Excitement mingled with curiosity as we stepped onto the land of enchantment. While our knowledge of Oslo was limited, we had a few plans in mind. The crisp air, tinged with a hint of frost, reminded us of the city's reputation for its cold and captivating beauty. Remember, here in Scandinavia, the sun only goes down for four hours a night.

One of our most anticipated visits was to the Contiki Museum, a treasure trove of Scandinavian history. As we stepped into its hallowed halls, we felt we had traveled back to a time surrounded by artifacts that spoke volumes of the Viking era. Ancient swords and shields adorned the walls, telling tales of brave warriors who once roamed these lands. The air crackled with a sense of adventure and the echoes of their journeys. Just a stone's throw away, we found ourselves in another realm from the past existence of the Viking Ship Museum. Here, we stood before the mighty vessels that had carried fearless Vikings across treacherous seas. The intricate craftsmanship of these ships left us to wonder if the spirits of their long-forgotten owners still lingered among us.

The Oslo Opera House stood out from the crowd. It was specially designed so visitors can walk on its rooftop. Oslo was a small, sleepy, noiseless city, and we found two days was enough to see what we wanted to see as this place was visited for its modern architecture.

Once again, we were on the move early in the morning to Stockholm, Sweden, a four-hour train trip away from Oslo. We arrived for our three-day stay before our upcoming Baltic cruise. We would depart from Stockholm on board the Royal Caribbean cruise ship, the Serenade of the Sea.

In the historical city of Stockholm, we found ourselves once again in the magic of music. The Abba Museum is a shrine dedicated to the legendary Swedish quartet. Stepping into the museum, we were immediately drawn into the world of Abba. The air was filled with their timeless hits, taking us to a time when disco reigned supreme. Memorabilia adorned the walls, showcasing the group's rise to fame and their lasting impact on the music culture.

Interactive exhibits invited us to become a part of Abba's story. We donned virtual reality headsets and found ourselves transferred onto the stage of their highly entertaining concerts, the crowd cheering and singing along. It was a moment of pure magic, a chance to experience the energy and excitement that surrounded this legendary band. As we wandered through the museum, we discovered personal belongings from each member of Abba. Benny's piano, Frida's stunning costumes, Agnetha's handwritten lyrics, and Bjorn's cherished guitars all held a piece of their identities. It was as if the essence of Abba lingered within these artifacts, connecting us to their journey and inspiring us to dream.

For now, our lives were that of two honeymooners living a quiet life of travel, and we enjoyed this time of peace and harmony. Everywhere we visited, from The Royal Palace to the Old Town to the many museums, we held hands tight without a care in the world. We wondered what our upcoming cruise would bring to the abundant travel experiences that we learned from our encounters with many different old-world cities.

Now, it was time to make our way to the cruise boat for a Baltic cruise. Horns blew, and passengers cheered, and Jane and I looked at each other with passion and kissed as Stockholm faded out of our sight. We departed this old, isolated city onboard our cruise boat, but we would return in seven days. This was our third time cruising, and the ship was perfect, with three buffets a day. The entertainment onboard was world-class, and even though we had an indoor room, it did not matter because the only time we were in the room was to sleep.

We stopped the first day at Visby, Sweden, a former Viking stronghold in years gone by. This town featured cobble-stone footpaths and fascinating ruins. Jane and I hung out in a coffee shop as the rain was coming down in buckets. We did not mind chatting with the Swedish people, who are warm and sweet, and between rain showers, we were still able to see the historic ruins that were still here as they have been for centuries. The Visby Cathedral, Town Hall, and Saint Nicolai Ruin were the three main features.

Tallinn, Estonia, was our next stop early the following day. This is the capital of the Baltic Sea. The country's cultural hub, with its walled perimeter with a 15th-century defensive tower. Once again, we roamed the cobblestone streets and appreciated the old-fashioned style of the city. Then, back on the ship, we got organized and were excited for our next two-day stop at sunrise in Saint Petersburg, Russia. We booked a hotel in town so we could have two full days to explore and mingle with the Russians.

The sun began to rise over the grand city of Saint Petersburg, Russia, casting a golden glow upon the glistening Neva River. Excitement buzzed through the air as Jane and I left the ship, ready to absorb ourselves in the architecture and the high-spirited culture. Our hotel, nestled in the heart of the city, offered a perfect base for our explorations. From there, we ventured out into the streets, eager to mix with the locals and discover the hidden gems that this enchanting city had to offer.

The first day was dedicated to exploring the magnificent landmarks that defined the imperial beauty of Saint Petersburg. We marveled at the glorious Winter Palace, standing proudly at the edge of Palace Square. The Peter and Paul Fortress beckoned us with its ancient fortifications and the striking golden spire of this remarkable Cathedral. Saint Petersburg, with the infrastructures from the past centuries, was breathtaking, maybe even more beautiful than Paris, but the gorgeous blonde Russian girls were our favorite attraction. We loved the attitude of the girls here as they were welcoming and over-friendly, which made the love birds attracted to their beauty.

The evening unfolded, and we found ourselves at an old pub drinking with the locals. We touched, we danced, we kissed, and then said our farewells to these fantasy pin-up girls. They asked to meet us again tomorrow night, but sadly, we have to be back on the cruise boat by the next afternoon, ready to set sail. That night, Jane and I were so passionate, and maybe both of us had fantasies of a Russian girl. As the sun began to set, we realized that our time in Saint Petersburg had come to an end, but our hearts were filled with gratitude for the moments of surprise, the sights and sounds that had ignited our senses.

As we boarded the ship once more, bidding farewell to this captivating city, we carried with us the spirit of Saint Petersburg. This city had opened its doors, allowing us to become a part of its story, if only for a fleeting moment in time.

Our last stop was Helsinki, the capital of Finland, and our boat was parked a long way from town. We walked for two hours around the picturesque and untouched lake, like two love birds keeping watch on the wildlife living on this calm lake before arriving two hours later in the city. Helsinki was a lot more modern-looking than our last stops. The central avenue, Mannerheimintie, is full of institutions, including the National Museum, tracing Finnish history from the Stone Age to the present day. The imposing Parliament House and the red-bricked Uspenski Cathedral overlook the harbor. We then got a local bus back to the boat as our feet were aching from excessive walking.

Life moves on, and another day in our lives comes to an end. Our day in Helsinki was a romantic special day where we saw sights firsthand that you only read about in the archives. The following day, we arrived back in Stockholm, and then we headed to the Stockholm Arlanda Airport, where we had one night hanging out in an old 747 that was transformed into a hotel and restaurant. This was an experience well worth having as we were drinking beers and eating our dinner on the massive wing of the plane all the time, secretly hoping the plane was indeed out of service and the plane would not take off.

Nightfall painted the sky with colors of purple and gold, and it was time to retire to our intimate quarters within the old Boeing 747. The gentle hum of the plane's aviation echoed around us as we drifted into an undisturbed sleep, safe in the knowledge that our flying dreams would remain grounded.

In the morning, we bid farewell to our temporary abode, our souls forever imprinted with the memories we had created within those nostalgic walls. And so, our time at the transformed airplane hotel came to a close, leaving us with a tale to share - a tale of experiences, of dining amidst the skies, and of dreams that were meant to stay earthbound.

Chapter 23

MOSCOW.

The following day, we were on a two-hour flight to Moscow, Russia, for eight great exciting days, and once we landed, our passports were checked for a valid visa. Then, with a welcoming smile, a stamp was inked inside our travel documents, granting us entry into this mesmerizing land.

We ventured beyond the airport's boundaries. We spotted a local bus, ready to transport us further into the heart of the city. The bus rumbled along, carrying us towards the Metro station, where we would begin our exploration of Moscow's marvel. As we emerged from the underground depths, the cosmopolitan feel of Moscow began to captivate us. We navigated through picturesque streets and winding alleys until we reached our temporary sanctuary - the Marriott Grand Hotel. Nestled on Tverskoy Street in the heart of the city center, it stood as a beacon of luxury and splendor.

We settled into this grandeur hotel and rested well. We had many plans for Moscow and wanted to be fresh for our first day. I looked Jane in the eyes and said in Russian, "Ya lyublyu tebya," meaning I love you. In Russia, they say this is expressed only when you are sure and want to confess your true love. I was one hundred and one percent sure, so it seemed appropriate to confess to my true love, Jane.

With hearts brimming with love and excitement, we set out to explore the wonders of this city. We walked down to Red Square and went for a tour to check out the train stations, which were like museums. At every stop, we were given a history lesson, and we saw more architecture and beauty, which was terrific. Next, we visited the Kremlin and Gorky Park. These places, with their buildings and structures, were something we never thought we would see in our lifetime. Here we were, visiting places that we had only seen before in movies; to see up close was a dream come true. This is the way my life took me now, just living the dream with the girl of my dreams.

It was now sunset as we walked back to our hotel and had an early dinner. Jane and I wanted to mix with the locals as all day, we saw beauty the same as we saw in Saint Petersburg. The song says, "Moscow girls really knock you out." And yes! We were overwhelmed by how lucky we were to be here. Soon, we found a small, cozy bar and ordered two Moscow Mules. Even though the drink originated in Los Angeles, America, I mean, what else would you drink in the place that a cocktail was named after?

A beautiful blonde girl was looking at us, maybe surprised as we were not Muscovites. She approached us and introduced herself as Sonja in a sweet voice with a strong accent. She told us she was originally from Siberia, a cold, isolated place in Russia, but had been in Moscow now for eight years. We shared some drinks with our new friend and then said warm farewells to Sonja and planned to meet her again tomorrow for dinner.

Sunrise and a new day were dawning with a clear but cold day to greet us in this city of beauty. Jane and I went out and about without a care in the world, just a little hungry for sightseeing. It was good now that we had a friend, and her local knowledge was welcomed. Jane and Sonja were able to text each other by trading numbers last night. Her guidance was so helpful, and she explained the do's and dont's in Moscow. Here, I would say only thirty percent of people spoke English, so it was difficult sometimes to communicate.

We ended up at Ploshchad Revolutsii train station, where we rubbed the nose of the lucky dog for good luck. We then spent our afternoon at the Old Arbat markets to the West of the Kremlin Wall. This street ran for one kilometer and sold unique goods, some only seen in Russia. We stocked up on some Russian dolls and then discovered a local coffee shop to rest our feet after a long day of walking.

As the clock struck 5 p.m., Jane's phone chimed with a photo text from Sonja. A smile tugged at our lips as we gazed at the image of Sonja and her friend Natalie, their faces filled with warm anticipation. It was a visual reminder of the dinner plans we had made earlier in the day. We couldn't help but feel a surge of excitement, knowing that the evening held the promise of not only delicious food but also delightful company. As the clock ticked closer to 7 p.m., our hearts beat with a mixture of excitement and nervousness. We stepped out of the hotel, ready to anticipate the unknown, eager to meet Sonja and Natalie and to allow the night to unfold.

The air was crisp, carrying whispers of distant music as we made our way to the designated restaurant. With each step, our anticipation grew, mingling with the buzzing energy of the city. And there, standing amidst the crowd, were Sonja and Natalie, their smiles radiant and infectious. Greeting each other with warm hugs and smiles, we instantly felt a connection, as if fate had brought us together for a purpose. The walls of the restaurant echoed with animated conversations, the clinking of glasses, and the aroma of delectable cuisine. The world around us blurred as we delved into stories and experiences, blending our voices and creating a symphony of friendship.

We were seated at a small but very well-decorated restaurant designed with the nostalgic past in mind. I allowed the girls to order the food, and Pelmini, the national dish of Russia, was ordered with a bottle of red wine. The dish was pastry dumplings filled with minced meat and wrapped in thin pastry-like dough. The food was filling, and before long, we were on our second bottle of red wine.

As the night unfolded, time seemed to lose its hold on us, dissolving into the realm of forgotten worries and cherished memories. The dinner that started as a mere plan had transformed into an enchanting evening filled with laughter and the beauty of human connection. Jane and Sonja seemed to like each other, and Natalie, the other Russian beauty, smiled at each other as we noticed their connection. Natalie was holding my hand, and then we were escorted back to our hotel. Little kisses were given as we said goodnight and invited the two girls to come to our hotel for drinks tomorrow evening, which they accepted excitedly without any hesitation. My life with Jane was exciting, and we both loved the way we never became jealous of each other, even though sometimes we flirted with other girls for fun. Jane and I made passionate love all night and were awake early for another day in Moscow.

This city was like time stood still, and this could easily be the 1800s instead of the 2000s. A river cruise on the Moskva River, where the capital gets its name, is the main river in the city, and it is a tributary of the Oka River where it flows. Jane and I enjoyed our panoramic river cruise, but it was becoming late, so we made our way back to the hotel to once again meet our Russian beauties at 7 p.m.

My mind was wandering around and thinking of different fantasies. Still, I remained calm and never had expectations of anything else except a few drinks, a bit of food, and a pleasant conversation. We sat at the hotel bar, awaiting our guests to arrive. Jane received a text that our guests had arrived, and when she went to meet them at the front foyer entrance, I ordered four Moscow Mules. I thought to myself to let this party start, as from life's experiences, a few drinks make an excellent start to the night.

I was sitting waiting in anticipation, and then three beauties came into view. I did not fall off my chair, but I had to hold on tight to my chair's armrests as maybe I would have. So, there we sat sipping on our drinks while talking small talk, and before long, another four Moscow Mules were ordered, and after that, another four. Sonja then asked me, to my surprise, if I would show her to the restroom, and I said, "Sure!" When out of sight of the other girls, she kissed me and asked if she could use the toilet in our hotel room as she did not like public toilets.

Ah, the twists and turns of fate that take us by surprise, steering our lives onto unforeseen paths. As Sonja and I slipped away from the table in search of a more private setting, little did we know that this impulsive decision would forever alter the course of our evening. The allure of Sonja's request intrigued me, her desire for privacy becoming a veil for something far more intimate. We stepped into the elevator and the anticipation palpable in the air as our lips met in a passionate embrace. Time seemed to stand still, our hearts racing as desire fueled our every move.

Inside the hotel room, the atmosphere crackled with electricity. Sonja sat delicately on the toilet, her presence captivating my attention. The intensity of the moment grew as our bodies became entangled, the softness of her neck yielding to my kisses. Pleasure mingled with the thrill of secrecy, heightening our connection. With the gentle touch of a lover, Sonja freshened herself up while I watched, my gaze fixed upon her reflection. The unspoken understanding between us only fueled the flames of desire, so we returned downstairs, our steps light and hearts ablaze.

To my astonishment, as we rejoined the table, Jane and Natalie were lost in their world, their hands clasped tightly, their eyes locked in a deep connection. It was as if time had paused for them, oblivious to our absence. Not a word was exchanged about our prolonged absence, and I wondered if they had noticed at all. Surprise and suspense now hung in the air, swirling around the four of us like a delicate dance. Had our actions shifted the dynamic of the evening? Would the bond between us be strengthened or shattered by our clandestine encounter?

As the night progressed, the unanswered questions played on my mind, weaving an intricate tapestry of emotions. The story of this evening had taken an unexpected turn, a twist in the plot that left us yearning for resolution. Little did we know that this moment of passion and secrecy would come to define not only this night but also the path our lives would ultimately take. The choices we made and the desires we succumbed to would ripple through the days and months that followed, forever altering the course of our beautiful relationships. And so it was, as the nights unfolded in Moscow, that the four of us found ourselves immersed in a tale of passion and connection.

The following night arrived, and with it, a shift in dynamics. The girls had booked a room in our hotel, an unspoken invitation for deeper exploration. Sonja and I found solace in one another's arms, our bodies tracing the contours of desire. Jane, in turn, sought comfort with Natalie, their connection blossoming within the confines of another room. But the nights that followed painted a different picture as the boundaries between us blurred, and our hearts warmed. A single bed became the sanctuary for our shared intimacy, where the warmth of our bodies mirrored the depth of our emotions. In this tangled web of passion, there were no rules, only surrender to the captivating pull of affection. Days were spent together in the unforgettable city of Moscow as a quartet. The bond between us grew stronger, bolstered by the shared experiences and the deepening connection that defied societal norms.

As the time to bid farewell approached, Sonja and Natalie drove us to the airport, their presence a bittersweet reminder of the transient nature of life's chapters. Warmth radiated in our farewells and gratitude. And as our plane took off from Moscow, Jane and I shared a quiet moment, gazes locked and hearts overflowing. In that fleeting instant, we found the true meaning in the language of love, softly whispering "I love you" in Russian, knowing that no matter what awaited us beyond the clouds, our story had forever been shaped by the love we discovered amidst the streets of Moscow.

I could reminisce all day and night about this city where the people were friendly, the girls were naughty, and the hotel we stayed in was second to none that I had ever visited before. One thing is for sure, we hoped that Jane and I could return one day. Sonja and Natalie have planned to see us both again in the future. We do not know where or when, but that day will one day come.

Chapter 24

The Philippines.

The next stop was Manila. A long flight of ten hours from Moscow to Singapore, then changing planes for three more hours flying time to Manila. Jane and I watched a movie and savored our dinner onboard before I slept with Jane in my arms. We planned to stay for a month in the Philippines and explore this country from top to bottom. We had a four-day booking in the Manila Hotel, an old and famous hotel where General MacArthur stayed during the Second World War.

Navigating the roads in the Philippine's capital city was no easy task. The streets seemed to be in a constant battle with the ever-increasing number of vehicles that clamored for space. Amidst the chaos of honking horns and stalled vehicles, there was an undeniable charm that seeped through the cracks. The resilience and resourcefulness of the Filipino people shone through as they maneuvered through the maze, finding alternate routes and shortcuts known only to them.

The bad driving habits of some may have added to the traffic woes, but it was also a reflection of the city's lively and passionate spirit. Crossing lanes with seemingly reckless drivers navigated their way forward, fueled by a determination to reach their destinations. The "Jeepneys" were the main public transport for locals, which were long vehicles painted in many bright colors; the more attractive they were, the more people would want to ride in them. They also had loud music playing and had open-air windows with bench seats on each side of the rear section, and these jeepneys would continually stop in the middle of the roads to pick up and drop off their passengers. So, all together, the traffic situation here was chaos.

We finally arrived at the Manila Hotel. Once we entered, I was amazed at the feel of this sophisticated hotel with a view of the magnificent bay and a combination of extraordinary beauty and warm service. Manila Hotel was not only a hotel, but it was carved in history, especially visited by the Beatles, which caused a diplomatic incident. The decorations and memorabilia from the floor to the ceiling were the best I had ever seen anywhere in the world. The staff was also dressed for the part to complement the decorations. In pure white pants and shirts for boys with white caps, the girls were dressed in traditional Philippine dress, which was befitting to the historical feel and setting.

We checked into this amazing hotel, and I felt overwhelmed that I had the chance to see and sleep under the ceiling of this museum-like residence. It was twenty-four hours since we left Moscow, so the travelers were exhausted and suffering from red, bloodshot eyes and weakened bodies. We slept for eight hours and woke the next day ready to explore this Wild West country called the Philippines.

On the lovebird's first day, we walked up to Rizal Park, which was named after the Filipino hero Jose Rizal. This hero was incidentally buried in this sixty-hectare significant urban park. The locals called it Luneta Park, which was its original name and was located in Ermita, about a ten-minute walk from the hotel. We walked around in this park like newlyweds for a few hours and then lay in the sun on the grassy lawns for a while. It was so vast and quiet that this park gave me the feeling like it was a Persian garden where a nightingale was singing with the rhythm of my heart, feeling the soft breeze dancing with the leaves wildly. I thought I traveled away with my mind to merge with the clear blue sky. We ended up napping under one of the shady trees, which were vast and plentiful in this magnificent park. The day went very quickly in a beautiful harmony without caring too much about the physical life.

The following day, the warm sun greeted us as we eagerly gathered outside our hotel with anticipation buzzing in the air. A van soon arrived, ready to whisk us away on our much-anticipated adventure. Today, we were on a journey to Corregidor Island, a place steeped in tales of resilience. As we boarded the ferry, joining other eager travelers, I couldn't help but feel a sense of reverence. Corregidor Island held a significant place in Manila's past, a testament to the challenges faced during World War II. It was here that General MacArthur, a symbol of courage and determination, made his stand against the advancing Japanese forces.

The island, perched at the entrance of Manila Bay, served as a strategic military stronghold. We stepped off the boat, our footsteps echoing against the remnants of fortified structures and bombed buildings. The island had witnessed the horrors of war, yet it stood as a testament to the indomitable spirit of those who fought for freedom. Plunged with the echoes of the past, the visit opened our eyes to the sacrifices made by those who came before us. It was a reminder of the fragility of peace and the resilience of the human spirit. As we walked through the remnants of the hospital-turned-tunnels, the air became heavy with a mix of emotions - gratitude, sadness, and wonderment.

The day unfolded like pages in a historical novel, each site revealing a new chapter in Corregidor's story. We left the island with a deeper appreciation for the sacrifices made and the bravery shown by those who fought during those turbulent times.

Jane and I spent our next day checking out Intramuros - the Wall City that the Spanish fortified dating back to 1571. It was only a fifteen-minute walk from the hotel. On our way, I noticed a lot of young students around the area and saw that there were many colleges in the vicinity. I was strong and kept control of myself to not fall into the temptation of these pretty and friendly Filipinas. It was going all good, and we enjoyed our touring days as I learned more and more about Manila and its former times. Just like that, four days passed by in a flash.

To make the last night count, we decided to visit the Tap Bar on the ground level of the hotel and found a seat at the bar. There was a great traditional band playing, which consisted of a piano player, a bass guitarist, and some guitar players. All the instruments were acoustic and gave a smooth feel and sound. The vocalist was a classy-looking and elegant lady wearing a stunning black gown and high heels. Her hair and makeup were groomed to perfection. This lady, I would say, was about thirty years of age yet had a unique professional voice. It seemed that she had a lot of singing lessons when she was younger, judging from her extraordinary voice and vocal skills.

After the first set of songs, the elegant lady took a seat on the other side of the bar from us. I sent her a tentative wave and said, "Hello! You are an outstanding singer". She instantly replied, "Thank you," with a happy smile on her face. I then asked the barman to offer her a drink, which she happily accepted. And the next thing I knew, she was sipping on a cocktail. I was thinking more along the lines of a beer, but a lady of her prestige was not cheap. It looked like she was a little nervous, judging from how quickly she finished her drink. Little did she know that I was much more nervous than her, especially with my beautiful wife sitting beside me, and maybe she would think I was a flirt or a womanizer.

I went on to offer her another drink, and this time, she came over and sat beside us. Jane and the singer looked at each other and talked for a few minutes. After their talk, everyone was okay, and there was no jealousy or drama. I am not sure what was said, but everything was now clear, and we were all relaxed. The barman then served her another cocktail, which I realized was called a Pina Colada - the one that they mention in the song of the early 80s with the same name. The elegant lady barely had time to finish her third drink, and after some small talk, she was back on stage to continue singing like a songbird. In about forty minutes, she sang eight songs and then again took a seat beside us. She seemed pleased as another cocktail was waiting for her.

When I smiled at the other band members, they frowned at me in response while giving a disgusted look on their faces. I confirmed with the elegant lady that she was single and none of her band members had any personal relation-ship with her. I wondered why they gave us that look. Then again, maybe they were just some serious musicians, but by this time, we did not care, and it sure seemed neither did the elegant singer.

She was sitting between us both, and before she went for her next set of songs, Jane gave her a little kiss on the cheek to be sweet. I did notice that this set was not as good as the previous two, and her songbird voice was not reaching the high notes as comfortably as before. The band members also looked agitated at this point. After this set, she came back to drink her fifth pina colada cocktail, but who was counting? This time, all three of us were even holding each other and getting as close as ever. Before I knew it, we were kissing each other as though we were the only three in the whole room.

The band was on stage for the fourth and last set, and our singer-friend went up after being called twice. So, with one last kiss, she staggered toward the stage. At this point, her hair was becoming a little messy, and her makeup was in urgent need of a touch-up. But this elegant lady was on stage, trying her best to sing as well as she could while holding the microphone stand in a way that seemed she would fall if she let go. After only four songs, the band surrendered with embarrassment as our newfound friend had become very drunk. Her singing - to be polite, was a little out of key.

We were back together. And once again, she was sitting on her chair and drinking. Then, I ordered some food and three more drinks. I was surprised when she asked the waiter to deliver it all to our room. We never got around to drinking the last drink or eating any of the food, and we ended up having a passionate night together.

The following day, we took her for breakfast, and she was wearing her dark sunglasses. As we left the room, we noticed the food and three drinks at the front door. The lady in sunglasses was so shy, obviously due to last night's treat. Noticing her shyness, Jane and I both apologized, but she said we didn't need to as it was the most fun night she had in years. After having breakfast, we bid her farewell by giving her a sweet kiss goodbye. We then went back to our room, packed our bags, and checked out. Jane kissed me and said in a soft voice, "I love you, my naughty husband."

We now needed tranquility away from the chaos and noise of the bustling city. We boarded a bus bound for Batangas, a two-hour ride that would take us closer to our destination, Mindoro Island. The bus journey was filled with scenic views of verdant landscapes. Upon reaching Batangas, we eagerly boarded a boat that would ferry us across the waters to Sabang Beach on Mindoro Island. The gentle rocking of the boat mirrored the rhythm of our anticipation. It was as if each wave carried us further away from the noise and closer to the serenity we sought. Arriving at Villa Sabang, we were greeted by the tranquil atmosphere of a seaside village. Sabang Beach exuded an aura of calmness, its shores untouched by the fast pace of the outside world. Here, time seemed to slow down, granting us the opportunity to absorb ourselves in the present moment.

Our days were filled with leisurely walks along the beach, hand in hand, as the waves whispered their secrets to the shore. The sun's warmth caresses our skin, rejuvenating our spirits and allowing us to forget any worries. In this little piece of paradise, we found joy in simplicity. We reveled in the stillness, cherishing the moments of silence that allowed our minds to unwind. As the days unfolded, we realized that it was not the grandness of our surroundings that brought us peace but rather the presence of each other.

On our first night, we walked over to the main town of Sabang, which was only a ten-minute walk. Sabang was a small, quiet, and simple township where the locals always made us welcome. Also here, there were some small restaurants and bars which we planned to visit after dinner to see the entertainment. We went for dinner at Captain Greg's, where they served a barbeque-type dinner where you choose your steak, chicken, or fish, and the salad bar was included for free. We ate our healthy, delicious dinner with some sweet red wine and relaxed with the rhythm of the ocean, feeling its gentle breeze.

Leaving Captain Greg, our curiosity led us to a noisy bar that seemed to pulse with a wild side of life. As we entered, the air was thick with anticipation, the beat of the music luring us closer to the heart of the action. The bar was adorned with flickering lights, casting an enchanting glow upon the stage. Here, young Filipina dancers moved with grace, their bodies intertwining with the poles as if they were born to defy gravity. Their performances, akin to that of circus acrobats, left us mesmerized.

The following day, I kissed my dearest Jane, and we walked over to a place called Big La La Goona, as the locals called it, where we planned to eat breakfast. The place was very calming, surrounded by nature, and on every side, you could find plenty of coconut trees and a calm ocean. Jane and I needed a very calm day to breathe fine and enjoy the little things the island had to offer. We strolled for twenty minutes on a pleasant walk from Villa Sabang, and on the way, we stopped to buy some locally made bracelets and T-shirts for some souvenirs. The sun was brightening, with Jane lighting up my life with her existence like an ocean of love. We had a very satisfying morning with an excellent healthy breakfast at the restaurant at Big La La Goona and then walked back to Sabang Beach.

On our way back to our hotel, a boat owner approached us, asking if we would like to hire him and his boat for the next day. He said, "Would you like to visit White Beach and island hop for the day?" This sounded like a great idea, so we both said "Yes!" with great excitement. We then agreed on a price with the respectful man. We arranged to meet up at 8 a.m. the following day in front of Villa Sabang. The night came very fast, and we just did our usual things with love and peace. It was heaven on earth with Jane.

After a good night's sleep, the morning came around, and sure enough, here was the boat, as the owner had been waiting for us and ready for our days traveling around the island of Mindoro. The boat, humble yet sturdy, navigated through the waters effortlessly. Our captain, perched at the back, guided us with expertise using a wooden rudder. The simple yet effective design of the boat, with its canopy made of wood and bamboo poles, lent an air of authenticity to our voyage. As we sailed on, new islands emerged on the horizon, each one a miniature paradise waiting to be discovered. We gazed at the lush foliage that adorned their shores, the mixture of colors blending seamlessly with the turquoise waters that embraced them.

Time seemed to slip away as we hopped from one island to another, each stop presenting its unique wonders. With every new destination, our spirits soared, the beauty of nature leaving an indelible mark upon our hearts. And so we continued our journey, entranced by the simplicity of life on the open sea. The boat carried us, not just from one island to another, but on a journey of self-discovery and appreciation for the world around us. We snorkeled until the day turned to night, and the darkness was upon us. We then set sail home for the final time, sunburned and tired from a great day out.

We bid farewell to the boat and its owner. Gratitude filled our hearts for the perfect day we shared. For in that small, humble vessel, we had found so much more than a mode of transportation. We had discovered a connection to the beauty of the world and a reminder that true joy lies in embracing the simplicity of life's journey.

Chapter 25

The Pregnancy.

The next day, we headed back to Manila after a romantic time on Mindoro Island. Then we traveled up to La Union, the Surf Capital of Luzon, where we stayed at a little surf camp just West of San Fernando, six hours North of Manila by bus. I spent my time here surfing and becoming tanned in the warm sun. Once again, we had the pleasure of coming across many friendly locals.

After a few days, we were off again, and our next stop was Baguio, the Summer Capital of the Philippines. The trip was taken up the mountain from La Union. The city of Baguio was always cold, with a harrowing journey for one hour driving up a steep and mountainous narrow highway, giving the driver no room for error - as an accident here was not even an option. The drop was straight down, with no chance of survival if we left the road. I nervously rode every corner on the mountain climb and sometimes closed my eyes when an overtaking car or bus just had time to get back on the right side of the road before hitting head-on with an oncoming vehicle.

And after a nerve-wracking bus ride, we arrived safely. It seemed that all the praying by the passengers had worked. We were staying at the Swagman Hotel. This hotel was warm and inviting, and we spent our nights sitting by the open fire, listening to the band playing love songs.

In the heart of Baguio's Burnham Park, amidst the lush greenery and serene lakes, we found ourselves hiring a rowboat and slowly glided across the glassy water. The sun gently touched our skin as we loved the tranquil lake that lay at the park's center. I could not help but start singing "Michael Row Your Boat to Shore," with Jane joining the chorus. How corny I had become, but I guess this is what love can do to a man when he feels captivated by his wife. Then, we hired a couple of bikes and rode them around the park until dusk. Generally, we just liked feeling young in this mountain city, and it was a good break away from the hot climate below. I had a lot of fun with my easy-going, happy wife, boating and riding bikes along the park.

Flying back to Manila was a fifty-minute flight to avoid the eight-hour bus ride. As we boarded the Asia Spirit plane, a sense of unease settled on my shoulders. The small propellers started, and with a sudden jolt, the aircraft taxied and began its ascent. At that moment, my heart skipped a beat as I saw the towering peaks of the mountains rushing closer, almost grazing the plane's wings.

Fear gripped me, realizing just how perilous this flight could be. Thoughts of the recent tragedy haunting my mind, where an Asia Spirit plane had crashed into the very mountains we were now flying over. The news of the thirty-six lives lost sent a chilling shiver down my spine. As the plane soared higher, defying gravity, I couldn't help but be amazed at the breathtaking view below. The rugged mountains, draped in lush greenery, seemed to hold a mystic allure. It was as if nature itself whispered tales of both beauty and danger. As the flight continued, my anxiety slowly transformed into a sense of calm. Each passing minute brought me closer to safety. Perhaps it was not our time to go yet, despite the ominous shadows cast by recent events.

Finally, the plane touched down in Manila, delivering us safely to the ground. Stepping onto solid land, I emerged stronger, reminded of the unpredictability of life and the fleeting nature of our time on this Earth. The next stop was Boracay, a further one-hour flight after a four-hour stopover in Manila. We arrived late at this white sand beach location, and it was midnight before we slept after a day of travel.

Boracay is a small island in the Central Philippines well known for its resorts and white beaches. Sunrise arrived, and we were swimming in the crystal-clear waters, splashing around like kids do. After our fun swim was finished, we drank coffee at one of the numerous coffee shops on the beachfront, just savoring our moment of peace. We went island hopping again on our second day, similar to Sabang Beach.

Amidst the natural beauty of Boracay, an unexpected twist took hold of the journey. On the third morning, as the sun painted a glow of colors in the sky, a wave of illness swept over Jane. Within the confines of the bathroom, she succumbed to bouts of vomiting, her face filled with a mix of discomfort and confusion. The next day was the same thing as early morning. Jane was sick again, and this time, my mind wandered a little. "Could Jane be carrying life within her?". I was thinking, could she be pregnant, but I never shared my thoughts with her.

Tomorrow, we would fly to Cebu, which was the place where Magellan, the Spanish explorer, lost his life at the hands of the first Philippine hero warrior Lapu-Lapu, and then onto Bohol, our last destination in this country full of happy people who always smiled even though they had very few or even no possessions. Cebu is the second largest city in the Philippines, known as the Queen City of the South, the capital of the Visayan region. Jane and I saw all the famous sights: Magellan's Cross, Fort San Pedro, and the statue of Lapu-Lapu. We hired a car and drove to the highest point of the city, known as "Tops." Here, we tasted a traditional dinner of adobo chicken, which is chicken pieces marinated in soy sauce and spices.

We went to a pharmacy called Watsons, and I asked the assistant for a pregnancy kit. Jane looked surprised at my purchase, and then early next morning at our hotel, we tested my smiling wife. Jane held up the test kit and said the result was positive. It was something we did not plan, but also never took any precautions. Our smiles told all, and we both glowed with happiness, so there was no need to ask what we thought of the news; we would soon be parents.

As the sun began its descent, casting a mesmerizing glow upon the city, I gazed at my radiant wife. Her pregnancy, like a gentle secret between us, sparked dreams and hopes for the future. I caught a vision of my most profound wish - a daughter adorned with Jane's beauty and grace. The next day, we were on a fast boat called the Ocean Jet for a two-hour trip to our final destination, Bohol, home of the Chocolate Hills. We chose to stay at Bohol Tropics. I noticed that it was a native hotel-style resort. It was located on the edge of the water, and I liked this new location, as I always loved the simple, cozy places that offer this calmness and the feeling of being home. Where the palm trees exist, I existed. At night, we went for a tranquil dinner as we had a good talk about tomorrow's tour with the highlight of The Chocolate Hills.

The first stop of our tour was Panglao Island, where we swam and laughed, and I tried the local alcohol called "Tuba." Oh, that drink was playing in my veins, giving me feelings like it was a combination of dopamine and adrenaline - It was a fermented coconut drink that delivered a kick with every sip I took in. I never allowed Jane to try this drink as now she needed to be careful as she was carrying our baby inside her beautiful body.

The next stop was about forty minutes away - the Loboc River. On arrival, we could see miniature squirrels or little rat-like creatures in the forest on the banks of the river. These cute little creatures were known as "Tarsiers," and they proved to be a great addition to the already beautiful view of the forest and river. One of the main features of these cute little things called Tarsiers was their huge eyes. These eyes did not move, but they could see from side to side by turning their heads one hundred and eighty degrees in both directions. These creatures were unique to this part of the Philippines only, and at one stage, there were about eight of them crawling on my chest and shoulders. Luckily, they did not bite. After my play with the little creatures, it was time to hit the road again for the highlight of the trip – the wonderous Chocolate Hills.

Another forty minutes passed, and we arrived at our destination. We immediately got out of the car, and there we were, looking up at a gigantic set of stairs that seemed to ascend on and on toward the sky. It reminded me of the tale of Jack and the Beanstalk, and I hoped that no giant would appear and eat me at the top. Logically, of course, this was not going to happen. Without hesitation, we started climbing and passed hundreds of steps before finally reaching the top. I was breathing heavily, and my heart rate had elevated as well, but looking out from this high position, all of my exhaustion went away.

I was breathless, not only from the steep climb but from the fantastic sight right in front of my eyes. We were looking into the distance, and it was a breathstealer. The view left me speechless - I could see hundreds of little, big, and round hill formations as far as my eyes could see. Some hills were brown, some green, but all of them looked truly amazing. I had been to so many different land formations on this planet, but this one was so unique. I had never seen anything like this before, and I doubted if I would ever be able to see a better sight than this again.

The legend of the Chocolate Hills says that the hills came from two giants who started a war by throwing boulders at each other. This continued for days, but the boulders were left to form these hills that we can now view and appreciate. This might sound unbelievable, but a part of me believed that it was all true. This view looked too good to be all-natural; there had to be a story behind it. At the end of the day, whether this legend was true or not didn't matter. We felt privileged to have seen these unique hill formations, and that's all that mattered.

After a long gaze across the Chocolate Hills, we watched the sun begin to descend. It was now time to climb back down the stairs, and we stepped slowly, as a slip might cause a broken neck. Once we were finally back on the ground, we went back to the car and headed back to Bohol Tropics and packed our bags. We would have an early morning flight tomorrow to Ho Chi Minh City, Vietnam, via a stopover to change planes in Manila.

One month in this country was full of memories and fun, and now my smile was more extensive and more frequent, knowing we would have an addition coming soon. Our baby was growing day by day, and my wife's beauty was also becoming more and more noticeable.

Chapter 26

Ho Chi Minh, Vietnam.

We calmly and patiently survived the long check-in line. The good thing was that the airline crew onboard was very friendly with warm hospitality. After about a two-hour and thirty-minute flight with Philippine Airlines, the plane was touching down in Saigon. It is the largest city that has an irrepressible spirit and is also considered the heart of Vietnam, beating day and night. Youthful enthusiasm flew through my veins just like a wild river that made me excited to see this city. Vietnam had only been reopened for tourists, perhaps fifteen years earlier after the war that ended in 1975. So, with almost a century of colonialism and brutal conflict, I kept in mind the recent history.

We emerged from the airport terminal, my eyes scanning the crowd for a sign with my name. It had been a long journey, and I had booked an airport transfer ahead of time, saving myself the hassle of navigating unfamiliar transportation. Instantly, I saw a smiling Vietnamese man with black sunglasses, and he had a mustache. He was holding up a handwritten sign with my name written on it. I recognized my name clearly as the man holding the sign also noticed me quickly, like we did know each other before. His warm smile put us at ease despite being in a foreign land. As I greeted him, a wave of deja vu washed over me as if I had known this man in another lifetime.

After greeting each other with a firm handshake, he grabbed our bags and escorted us to his taxi, which was clean and smelt like new. I thought that he treated this taxi like it was his wife, with special care. Before long, we were on our way to town. The man skillfully navigating the chaotic streets of Saigon. As we weaved through traffic, he shared stories of his beloved city, bringing its past to present. The man's genuine warmth and unwavering hospitality made us realize that sometimes, the most meaningful connections can be forged within fleeting moments.

I was pleasantly surprised when we pulled up outside our hotel. The building where we were dropped off looked very nice with an elegancy which you can see in every part, and everything was well organized. It had an exquisite bar and restaurant on the rooftop with a fantastic view. The Rex Hotel was the name and was located in the middle of Red Square, as they called the area outside the hotel. Around Red Square were red communist flags with yellow stars and pictures of Ho Chi Minh, the leader of the country as drawn on banners - which was naturally the reason the name of the city was changed from Saigon to, of course, Ho Chi Minh City.

Coincidently, the day we arrived in the city was also Chinese New Year, which made me feel even more excited as there would be a lot of celebrations for the Year of the Dragon tonight. It was also relieving that the war here was over, and it felt like the future had arrived in this city. We walked up to the city center and noticed that many locals were also out and about. Crossing the road was going to be almost impossible, as hundreds or maybe even thousands of small motorbikes were six and seven abreast, flowing endlessly through the chaotic streets, beeping their horns in perfect harmony. At least, that is what they thought. We had no choice but to cross the road and so we did, finding ourselves dodging against the motorbikes all the way.

We reached the other side of the busy road, and it felt like we had just gone through a marathon, even though the boulevard crossing seemed endless. Such was the relief I felt to have conquered the motorbike gauntlet. We even threw our arms up and cheered like we had won the event. Then I looked around and found a street-chic bar, which seemed to be full of friendly people. So naturally, that was where we headed.

After finding a comfortable seat at the open-air bar, we sat down, and I rested my legs while I sipped on a cold and refreshing local beer, and Jane drank ice water. Soon, we began watching the amazing fireworks that were brightening the dark sky above. The youthful locals, with hearts full of vitality, cheered and hooted at every dazzling crescendo. Their joy echoed through the streets, intermingling with the crackling sounds of fireworks. It was a symphony of laughter and jubilation that enveloped the City of Saigon, weaving a feeling of simple happiness.

We were sitting and minding our own business when two pretty and friendly Vietnamese girls offered us a ride home. They had small motorbikes, and since we did not feel like walking, we happily accepted their offer. I noticed that the girl that I was riding with did not look pure Vietnamese and was half-American. She was very attractive - so much so that maybe in another life, if she was born lucky, she could have been an actress or at least a model. Well, she seemed happy just where she was for now. Jane and her driver were quickly going their way, and I said, "See you at the hotel, sweetheart," and then I told my driver my hotel name and sat on the back of her bike. Then she handed me a helmet, which, seeing the way the locals rode, I immediately placed on my head.

Unexpected twists can turn an ordinary evening into a tale of surprises and self-discovery. As we zoomed through the chaotic streets, an inexplicable deviation occurred. It was there that I discovered the nature of her occupation- a truth that caught me off guard. Perhaps lost in translation or simply a quirky twist of fate, she took me to a modest boarding house instead of my intended hotel. It was a small room with a mattress on the floor and a very small bathroom. This girl, after I took some time to look at her, was a real beauty queen. She also had the body of a model with a tiny perfect waist and very long beautiful legs and delicious thighs like a fresh French creme. I kept looking very slowly at this beauty.

I could not stop myself as I pinned her over the wall very gently, and I began to kiss her sweet lips slowly like Debussy was playing on the piano; her lips were shaped like a heart, and she was a flower without a heart. Then she took me in the shower, which was an exaggeration as it was just a hose from a faucet protruding from the wall. This girl washed me down well as the night smoke and my sweat needed to be washed from my body. I reciprocated and also washed the girl well. As we dried off, I started to kiss her again. I was so hard from her taste and slowly climbed on top of her, inserting myself deep inside. We made love and pleasured each other for the next two hours. I realized that it was time to leave, so both of us slowly got dressed and soon were back on the motorbike.

She dropped me at the front of my hotel, and I gave her a few more kisses before waving her goodbye. I did ask her to stay with me for the night, but she said that local girls were not allowed to stay in hotels with foreigners unless they were checked in on arrival. I told Jane all about my unexpected encounter with my lady motorbike driver. That night, I felt Jane was so horny after my stories of the sexual experience with the girl who had movie-star looks. It excited us both, and we made love until we finally fell into a deep sleep.

The next day, I woke up with a lot of energy, like a King who won a great battle. I rewarded myself with a healthy breakfast – taking in the happy morning, although for a while, I felt like I was in a movie; it was not reality. I smiled from the bottom of my heart, and then I said to myself, "Well, if it is a movie, then I am a great Director!". After breakfast, we went to Singh Café, which is a place where tourists and backpackers stay. It was similar to Khaosan Road in Bangkok. It was a mass of drinking bars, restaurants, and travel agents with tour operators. There, we were able to purchase a tour to explore the Cu Chi tunnels and relics of the Vietnam War, which I booked for the next day.

The tour operator arrived on time the following day. It was going to be about a two-hour van ride from the city. Before us stood remnants of a bygone era, relics frozen in time. Tanks, once menacing, now stood as solemn reminders of the violence that once consumed this land. But it was the small tunnels, hidden beneath the Earth's surface, that held the secrets of survival and resistance.

The Viet Cong, brave souls who called these underground chambers their home, knew the art of concealment like no other. In these tiny passageways, they lived, breathed, and fought. From these secret hideouts, they emerged like phantoms, where they would ambush the French and American soldiers during the war that nearly destroyed this country from 1955 to 1975. And most of them didn't know the main reason why they got involved in this brutal war. It was a struggle fueled by ideology, engulfing the lives of countless innocent souls thrown into the throes of battle. Poverty forced some to fight while others saw honor as their guiding light, unknowing of the true motives that had set the stage for destruction.

The tour was then completed with a short propaganda movie that they played during this period to brainwash the people and motivate them to fight the evil enemy. All in all, we enjoyed the day, and it was all well worth the experience. We arrived at our hotel after our exciting and informative trip, and we were exhausted.

The next morning, on our last day in Saigon, we were approached outside our hotel by a friendly old Vietnamese man with a rickshaw. He looked worn out, haggard, and sundried and had a thin body. He looked about sixty years of age, but maybe he was only forty. After a small conversation, I hired him for the day to show us around. We had taken an instant liking to this older man, and we were acting as if we were old friends. He took us to visit the war museum and a few other city tourist spots.

After some time going around the city, I suddenly started feeling guilty and offered the older man that I would be the horse for a while. He did not accept my request at first, but then, after some persuasion, he allowed me to be the driver of the rickshaw sometimes. I then realized, being the driver, how hard it was pulling the rickshaw in the Vietnam heat.

Jane and I, with our newfound friend, this old and simple Vietnamese man, were laughing at each other's jokes. Before we knew it, the night fell. I invited my guide to join us for dinner as a parting gesture. He humbly accepted my invitation, and we found a nice old-fashioned and French-styled restaurant to eat. It was by the Mekong River, and we sat outside and ate well. We also sampled the house's special Escargot, which was a dish consisting of cooked and edible land snails. We tasted this fine dish, and it was the first time that I had tried something as exquisite and delicious as this in my life.

We also savored a few beers together, and I could see how much he appreciated our company. We enjoyed our dinner with laughter, even though our conversations were pretty limited. And then, it was time to say our goodbyes to each other. We then gave him a friendly hug and handed him a good reward for his day's services and guidance.

Our Saigon trip had been memorable, and I knew that one day, we would return to this city and explore and spend more time here. Feeling tired, we went back to our hotel room early to rest as tomorrow we had another flight.

Chapter 27

Da Nang and Hanoi, Vietnam.

Da Nang is the central part of Vietnam. Here, we found ourselves captivated by the sandy beaches and the echoes of a colonial past. With our hotel overlooking the stunning beach, we wasted no time in embracing the seaside paradise. Minutes after dropping off our bags, excitement infused our every step as we raced toward the inviting waters. Like carefree teenagers, our laughter mingled with the crashing waves as we delighted in the simple pleasure of swimming in the warm embrace of the sea. We were immersed in the history of a place that once witnessed the strife of the Vietnam War, now transformed into a heavenly haven. This beach was called China Beach, the setting of the Vietnam War drama series running from 1988 to 1991.

With only a few precious days to explore, the afternoon beckoned us to venture further afield. The towering hilltop awaited our ascent, promising a breathtaking encounter with the giant guardian of Da Nang, Lady Buddha. We climbed higher, our steps inspired with anticipation. And there, amidst the clouds, stood Lady Buddha, a majestic figure reaching an astounding height of sixty-seven meters. Her serene presence enfolded the city below, her gaze eternal and compassionate. From this vantage point, we beheld a city steeped in pride and resilience. I felt Da Nang was more than just a destination; it was a city that possessed a feeling of calm and peace.

Jane and I crossed the Dragon Bridge, which is six-hundred-and-sixty-six meters long with six lanes of traffic. Having reached the other side of town, our weary bodies needed rest. The tranquil river banks were the perfect backdrop to plan the following day. The soft glow of streetlights danced on the water's surface as I indulged in the rewards of our travels with a few well-earned local beers, savoring each sip as we watched the world pass by. Jane was savoring ice-cold sparkling water that she told me tasted better than beer. I just smiled and never murmured a word. Our lives were just a travel dream, and with Jane's body now showing signs there was a baby inside, we needed to enjoy the next two weeks before we settled.

Early morning, we were now at the Marble Mountains, a cluster of five marble and limestone hills. Here, we spent hours slowly and carefully climbing through the network of tunnels with towers and pagodas built by Mahayana Buddhists and the Nguyen Dynasty Kings. The two climbers were exhausted, with every bone in our bodies aching from hours of climbing at this unique attraction.

On our last day, we visited Hoi An, a well-preserved ancient town about thirty minutes from Da Nang, cut through the canals. This old town was a step back in time. The authenticity of Hoi An resonated in every detail. From the traditional dress worn by locals to the ornate facades of restaurants and shops, every element exuded the sense of being transported to a past century. We strolled through the streets, marveling at the mixture of colors that adorned the buildings and the delicate lanterns that hung overhead, infusing the town with a warm and magical ambiance.

We discovered hidden gems tucked away amongst the historic buildings, a charming tea house serving fragrant brews, and a tailor shop with skilled artisans creating unique garments from the past. This day in Hoi An was not just a respite for our tired bodies but also nourishment for the souls. It was a chance to slow down to appreciate the beauty of a town frozen in time. The combination of ancient architecture, timeless traditions, and the heartfelt hospitality of the locals left a warm feeling in our hearts.

On the move, again, we were flying with Vietnam Airlines to Hanoi, the North of Vietnam and the capital of this beautiful old country. It is hard to believe a brutal war once destroyed so much and took so many lives, ending the destruction in 1975. Touching down in Hanoi, we found ourselves in a city that radiated a sense of resilience and vitality. Our accommodation was nestled within the ancient quarters, where the echoes of a thousand years reverberated through the narrow streets and bustling markets. Each step we took carried us through layers of the olden days, reminding Jane and I of the endurance and spirit of the Vietnamese people.

Excitement filled our hearts as we booked an overnight cruise in the breathtaking Halong Bay, a UNESCO World Heritage site renowned for its mystical limestone karsts rising from the emerald waters. The following day, at the early hour of 8 a.m., our transfer arrived, ready to whisk us away to a world of wonder and tranquility. As we began on the journey to Halong Bay, anticipation swelled within us. The ethereal beauty of the bay seemed to hold secrets waiting to be unveiled. The boat carved through the water, passing by awe-inspiring rock formations that stood tall, guardians of a hidden realm.

The overnight cruise was a symphony of surprises. We sailed amidst the floating villages, witnessing the everyday lives of the local fishermen and their families. And as the sun dipped below the horizon, we found ourselves surrounded by a peaceful calm, captured by the serenity of Halong Bay. As we traveled back to Hanoi, touched by the wonders of a magnificent bay that captured the way we both pictured this God-made planet, we knew that Vietnam would forever hold a special place in our hearts. And so, our love journey continued as we clenched each new adventure and allowed the stories of Vietnam to weave their way into the dreams of our lives.

Chapter 28

Cambodia and Bali.

It was an unforgettable time in Vietnam, a country that is serene and relaxed. Now Jane and I found ourselves soaring through the skies to Cambodia, the neighbor of Vietnam. This city was known as the home of Angkor Wat, which is located in Northwestern Cambodia.

As we touched down in Siem Reap, a sense of anticipation filled the air. We made our way to Pub Street, the entertaining heart of the city's nightlife. Backpackers and tourists alike converged here, drawn to the lively atmosphere that came alive as the sun began to set. Restaurants and pubs lined the one-hundred-meter stretch, each one offering its unique charm. After indulging in a simple dinner and savoring a cold beer, Jane and I decided to venture into the renowned Hard Rock Café. The sound of live music and nostalgia greeted our ears as we entered. The band playing was a throwback from the 60s with their infectious energy. We found ourselves drawn into the rhythm, immersed in the music until the late hours of the night.

Following a deep sleep filled with dreams that were hard to know the true meanings, the body of my darling wife Jane wrapped around me gave a contented feeling, but we had to move and were soon in a van at 9 a.m. for our tour. In this part of Cambodia, there are approximately fifty Buddhist and Hindu Temples dating back to the 12th century.

Angkor Wat was the most famous, and we explored the ruins for an hour, then onto Angkor Thorn, with over one hundred statues of Gods and Demons at the gates. Ba Yon Temple was next, which had fifty stone towers with intricate carvings made by talented craftsmen depicting the four faces of Bodhisattva Avalokiteshvara on most of them. Ta Prohm Temple was next on the agenda, made famous as the setting of Tomb Raider starring Angelina Jolie.

As the sun dipped below the horizon, casting a warm golden glow over the temples, Jane and I were overwhelmed by the beauty and grandeur of Siem Reap. After six hours of climbing through the ruins of temples, we were now back at our hotel, where we had an early night. We left Temple City behind, with new places waiting for us to visit. We were tired but very contented to see the temples and structures that time had forgotten in this land, where the past dwelled and spirits roamed. Tomorrow, we will take a 6 a.m. bus to board for a six-hour trip to Phnom Penh, the busy capital of Cambodia. This city sits on the junction of the Mekong River and Tonle Sap Rivers.

With a long trip ahead, we watched a movie on our computer called "First They Killed My Father," a story that was sad but gave us a little knowledge of this country's brutal past. Our long bus trip was ending, and we arrived in a busy, bustling city called Phnom Penh, the capital of Cambodia. An opposite atmosphere to Siem Reap, which was laid back and distinctive. We were tired by the time we checked into our hotel, and I just rested with Jane that even after our long trip, she still looked beautiful. I kissed her sweet strawberry lips, and we both fell into a deep sleep.

As the sun began to rise, we eagerly waited for our driver to take us on a tour that would reveal the hidden stories of Phnom Penh. Our first stop was the infamous S-21 prison, a place that held secrets and haunting memories within its somber walls. Once a school filled with laughter and hope, it had been transformed into a chamber of despair and anguish by the ruthless Pol Pot Regime. As we entered the premises, a heavy silence hung in the air as if the ghosts of the past were watching our every move. The desolate corridors echoed with the cries of the tortured and the innocent. Each room told a different story of pain and suffering as we saw the remnants of iron shackles and bloodstained floors. The walls themselves seemed to bear witness to the atrocities committed within their confines.

I couldn't help but feel a knot tighten in my chest, a mixture of anger and sadness that such cruelty could exist within the hearts of men. I cannot comprehend how humans could inflict such unimaginable suffering on their fellow beings. The photographs of the prisoners, worn and weathered by time, stared back at us with haunted eyes. Each face represented a life that was cut short, a story silenced in the depths of darkness. Their eyes seemed to plead for justice, for the world to remember their struggles and never forget the horrors they endured.

Leaving S-21, we carried the weight of their stories with us, a responsibility to honor their memory and ensure that such atrocities would never be repeated. As we continued our tour, the city took on a different shade, tinged with melancholy. Phnom Penh, a city of contrast and resilience, had witnessed unspeakable sadness. But within its streets, there was also hope and strength. Jane and I were shaken, and I had to comfort my darling as I noticed tears from her beautiful eyes, slowly running down her cheeks, forcing me to hold back my tears. Such was the effect on us both, and yet with the worst place to come.

We now stopped at the Killing Fields. Here, between 1976 and 1978, up to three million people were murdered by the Khmer Rouge government under Pol Pot. The hundreds of stacked human skulls for all visitors to see, and I held Jane tight as we listened to our guide's explanation. The silence was deafening in the air as we stepped onto the hallowed ground. A chilling breeze whispered through the tall grass, carrying with it echoes of the past. The field, once a place of tranquility, had been transformed into a site of unspeakable horror during the darkest days of Cambodia's history.

Rows of mass graves emerged before us, each containing the remains of countless innocent souls. The enormity of the tragedy unfolded before our eyes as we learned of the brutal acts committed within these very fields. The stories of those who had lost their lives here echoed in our minds, refusing to be forgotten.

The bones and clothing of the victims stood as a horrifying reminder of the atrocities that had taken place. As we walked around the grounds, we couldn't help but feel a profound sense of sorrow and despair. How could one person inflict such cruelty upon another? I held Jane close, but amidst the anguish, there was also a glimmer of hope. The resilience of the Cambodian people and their determination to rebuild and heal revealed itself in the whispers of recovery that surrounded us. It was a testament to the indomitable spirit of humanity.

Leaving the Killing Fields at nightfall, we soon arrived back in the city, and to cheer up, we visited the bars of Phnom Penh. We were toasting for the memories of the past murdered Cambodians whose bravery and fate, through no fault of their own, we wanted to remember them in high regard. Our last day in Phnom Penh was a quiet one as, once again, tomorrow, we would be on the move for our last stop, Bali, Indonesia, before returning home to Australia.

We landed at sunset and checked into our hotel called The Stones, directly across from the beach of Legian. The hotel also boasted a giant swimming pool, and we had a week to relax here. We needed to relax and clear our minds after a sad but well worth the visit to Cambodia. Daybreak and the surf were pumping, so I hired a surfboard and paddled out amongst the locals and visitors to enjoy the glassy waves of Bali. After all, this island resort was world-renowned for its surf beaches and reefs, so when in Bali, my idea was to enjoy what the island is famous for, and that was surfing.

After two hours and with heavy, tired arms, I dropped the surfboard back to the happy, friendly Balinese man and thanked him warmly, and then went back to our hotel to enjoy happy hour by the pool. In between my surfing escapades, I would relax contentedly for hours. The warm sun kissed our skin as I sipped on refreshing Bintang beers, indulging in the carefree atmosphere of our honeymoon. However, for Jane, the delights of alcohol were off-limits due to her condition. But her joy was unwavering, and her presence alone brought me endless happiness.

As we bid farewell to Bali, eager to carry our memories with us, an unexpected hurdle awaited us at the airport. The stern-faced immigration officer demanded a health certificate before allowing us to board the plane. Panic crept in as we realized we hadn't obtained one. Feeling desperate, I approached a supervisor, slipping a one hundred dollar note into his hand, hoping it would sway his decision. Luck was on our side as the gift was accepted, and we were granted permission to depart on our journey home.

Sitting onboard the airplane, soaring through the sky at thirty-six-thousand feet, a mix of relief and nostalgia washed over me. I looked back on six months of travel, love, and adventures that most could only dream of. The unique landscapes, the mesmerizing temples, the times shared, and the unbreakable bond we forged. As I gazed out at the world below, I was filled with gratitude for the experiences we had lived, the love we had found, and the memories we would forever cherish. No amount of money, turbulence or distance could shake the foundation of the love we had built together. Benjamin Franklin once said "Whoever said money can't buy happiness isn't spending it right". Our journey may have come to an end, but our story was far from over.

Chapter 29

Gemelu

Touchdown at Brisbane International Airport was rough. The wheels of the plane screeched upon landing, causing a jolt that shook Jane to her core. Shock surged within me, but it was soon soothed by the captain's humble apology over the intercom. A small gesture, perhaps, but one that couldn't be refused.

We gathered our bags and made our way to the car rental counter. It was time to return to our humble abode, nestled in front of the tranquil Brisbane River. The cupboards were bare, so we made a stop at the grocery store to stock up on food. It had been over six months since my life took a remarkable turn. Back then, I was a solitary, carefree man, drifting through each day without any plans for marriage or children. And now, here I stood, a married man eagerly awaiting the arrival of a precious baby. Tomorrow was a big day for us; we had a doctor's appointment to check on the well-being of our little one.

As Jane drifted off to sleep, I watched her dream, amazed at the beautiful transformation that love had brought into my life. My hand gently caressed her stomach, filled with an overwhelming tenderness that only true love could evoke. I prayed silently, hoping that everything would be alright with our baby. Tomorrow held the answers we longed for.

The morning arrived, brimming with anticipation. We made our way to the doctor's office, our hearts racing with excitement and trepidation. Our appointment with the doctor was at 9 a.m., but we arrived early and were sitting while looking into each other's eyes like we just met and were curious about what we were both thinking. Then suddenly, we heard a voice saying, "Jane, come inside." We stood up with excitement but concern, and once inside the doctor's room, we both sat with a smile. The doctor said, "How can I help you?" His eyes looked confused when I said, "I think my wife is pregnant, and we need to make sure all is ok." Doctor Timmins was his name, and he said in a firm voice, "Upon my observation, she is at least six months pregnant," and followed with a question. "Who is the doctor have you been seeing?" I said, "You are the first doctor, as we have traveled the world for the past six months." His face then turned to disappointment as he felt the stomach of Jane and checked her blood pressure and the baby's heartbeat.

A wave of realization washed over us. We had been so consumed by our whirlwind adventures, traveling across the globe, that we failed even to consider seeking medical care during this precious time. The disappointment on Doctor Timmins's face mirrored our own. Yes, maybe thinking back, we should have stopped traveling and been home months earlier, but we were so enthralled in our life we never even thought about our insanity.

Without wasting another moment, he picked up the phone and urgently requested an appointment with an OB gynecologist. As he instructed us not to travel any further, his voice dripped with sarcasm, subtly highlighting our foolishness. Grateful for his assistance, we thanked Doctor Timmins and spoke to his secretary, who promptly arranged a 3 p.m. appointment with an OB-gyne specialist at the city hospital.

Doctor Croft would be the one to guide us forward. It was only 9:40 a.m., so Jane and I decided to drive back home and waited until 2 p.m. before driving into the city hospital. Entering the hospital, we made some inquiries and found Doctor Croft without too much problem. She greeted us warmly, her reassuring presence making us feel at ease. Following a similar procedure as Doctor Timmins, Doctor Croft conducted a thorough examination, even performing an internal check-up. She then informed us that an ultrasound was scheduled within the hour, conveniently located within the same hospital.

As we entered the ultrasound clinic, a sense of awe washed over us. The room was dimly lit, with a flickering screen monitor waiting for us. Our hearts raced with anticipation as the technician began the procedure. And there she was, our little miracle, displayed on the monitor. The technician announced with a smile, "You're almost seven months pregnant, and it's a girl." Jane's eyes shimmered with tears of joy, and I couldn't help but be overwhelmed with emotion. I held onto my sweetheart tightly, feeling the gentle movements of our daughter within Jane's expanding body. It was a moment of pure bliss, a fragment of time when everything felt perfect.

As we drove back home, the name "Gemelu" lingered in our minds. It encompassed the beauty of this unexpected journey, symbolizing the precious bond we shared as a family. We whispered the name softly, imagining the day when we would finally hold her in our arms. The adventure may have been unconventional, but the love that blossomed during our travels only served to magnify the joy awaiting us in the future. Life had taken us on a winding path, filled with surprises and twists, but as we looked toward the horizon, we knew that the arrival of Gemelu would be the greatest of them all.

The next coming weeks sped by like a flash filled with excitement and anticipation. We were now driving to the hospital as Jane's water had broken, contractions were getting stronger and more frequent, and the time had come for our little Gemelu to enter the world. The labor was intense, and Jane endured hours of pain. Nervous and anxious, I stood by her side, offering words of encouragement and support. And then, finally, after what felt like an eternity, our baby girl arrived, screaming her arrival to the world.

Gemelu was perfect, and I held her close to my body; her eyes were like little brown buttons, and her hair was wet and glistened in the light. I laid our baby on the chest of Mummy, and now and forever, it would be Jane and I and one extra in our life. The spoken words could not describe our total happiness. The sight of our beautiful daughter, the bond between mother and child was instant and profound, a connection that would endure for a lifetime. Our family had expanded, and from this point forward, it would be just the three of us sharing a love that words could never adequately express. As I gazed at Gemelu's features, I couldn't help but see the perfect blend of both Jane and myself. Her face carried a resemblance to us both, a unique mixture of traits that made her truly one of a kind.

In that hospital room, amid the exhaustion and exhilaration, I couldn't help but feel an overwhelming sense of gratitude. Our lives had been forever changed, enriched by the arrival of our precious Gem. And as we embraced the path that lay ahead, we knew that our love would guide us through every twist and turn, creating memories that would last a lifetime.

Gemelu would sleep with contentment, only stirring for the comforting warmth of her mother's milk or the tender touch of skin-to-skin cuddles from her daddy. This deep and unconditional love we felt for our daughter was unlike anything we had ever experienced before. It was the type of love that transcended words, only found in the pages of storybooks and fairy tales. It was a love that knew no bounds, guiding us through sleepless nights and challenging days with unwavering strength. We navigated the winding road of parenthood; we understood that the greatest satisfaction lay within the laughter, tears, and endless love we shared as a family.

Jane was now a beautiful Mummy, and I was the world's proudest Dad as we both cherished the next few months being parents and raising our little angel. All the travels, even to a nearby universe, could not give us more happiness or contentment than our parenthood. Every day was filled with wonder as we watched our precious daughter grow. She was still so small, but each passing day brought new milestones and discoveries. Our lives had transformed into something beautifully simple. No amount of worldly adventures or escapades could compare to the happiness and contentment we found in being parents. Our universe had shifted, and the newfound purpose that came with raising our daughter became our greatest source of fulfillment.

Chapter 30

The Final Twist

Three months went by, and Jane received a call from Yuli. She wanted to visit us in Australia. She also mentioned that she would not be alone and wanted to introduce someone very special to her. Jane had told Yuli we had a big surprise for her also. Intrigued and excited by her cryptic words, Jane and I eagerly awaited Yuli's arrival. As we awaited her visit, anticipation hung in the air with curiosity. What could be the surprise she had in store for us? We wondered, and our minds filled with a swirl of possibilities. Yuli's arrival stirred a sense of excitement and curiosity within us. Thoughts swirled through our minds, "Could she have found a boyfriend or perhaps even a husband?". Regardless, we awaited her arrival with open hearts, eager to share in her happiness.

Jane and I both loved Yuli and were happy for her, and she sounded very excited to see us, too. We were waiting for her exact arrival day, and then, on a Sunday afternoon, there was a buzz at our front door. We were a little startled as we never got a visitor, so I went and slowly swung open the front door. My astonishment peaked at the sight before me. There stood beautiful Yuli, radiating both nervousness and looking a little apprehensive, cradling in her arms a child boy of about the same age as our beloved Gemelu. With an overwhelming surge of emotions welling up inside, I refrained from asking any questions and instead hugged Yuli warmly. Jane mirrored my actions, allowing the love between us to flow. At that moment, no words were necessary; the unspoken understanding vibrated in the air.

Yuli then handed me the child and hugged Jane again with total love, and then Jane introduced Gemelu with surprise on her face, equaling the surprise on our faces. Jane and I asked what her son's name was and observed that Yuli seemed hesitant to talk. Yuli's hesitation to speak about her son became now more apparent. She appeared to be carrying a weight, a story yet to be told. We respected her silence, allowing her the time and space to share when she was ready. The atmosphere remained gently charged, brimming with unspoken questions.

We all then sat down, and silence was now echoing through the house. The two babies were now lying beside each other, looking very similar. We then waited in anticipation for Yuli to tell her story to us. Yuli then said, "His name is Geoff; I named him after his father." I said, "Wow! Same name as me? And his father's name is Geoff also?". Just then, my brain and mind opened up, and I realized the boy had an identical look to Gemelu. I then realized this was my son, and without confirmation, I picked up this boy again with the same name, and I said to him, "My name is Dad," as tears of emotion flowed from my eyes.

Yuli then said, "Yes, Geoff, you are the father," and started to make an apology, but I cut her words and said, "Now I was double happy with a four-month-old boy and girl." Gemelu was a mere four days older than my junior Geoff. Jane's face lit up with sheer happiness at the arrival of her son and daughter, and Yuli was equally delighted to have expanded our family once again. It felt as if we were living in a story that one would only expect to see on television, like a feature on Sixty Minutes. I couldn't help but smile, overwhelmed with gratitude for the blessings that filled our lives.

In the following week, we ventured out to buy another crib and a double pram, along with an array of tiny clothes for our newest addition. The shop attendants were taken back, their faces a picture of bewilderment as they witnessed me caring for two babies. Perhaps they assumed they were twins. I thought optimistically. Yet deep down, I knew that people weren't naive and could undoubtedly discern the truth that I had two wives. But times were changing, and the world we now lived in was more accepting and tolerant than ever before. It no longer mattered what others might think or assume.

Our family defied societal norms and embraced the beauty of our unconventional situation. I found total contentment in the fact that I had been named as Geoff's father on the baby's birth certificate, allowing me to facilitate his Australian citizenship. With Yuli's permanent residency secured, our family flourished in our new, spacious home. It felt as if we were living in a dream, each day filled with love and laughter. My heart swelled with affection for my two children, Geoff and Gemelu, as the years flew by in a blur of cherished memories.

As their early years passed, the time came to enroll Geoff and Gemelu in school. We stood before the admissions office, faces beaming with pride yet also with a touch of curiosity. The school administrator spared no questions, their expressions betraying a mixture of surprise and intrigue. Little did they know that our unique family held even more surprises in store. For you see, as we walked through the school corridors on that first day, pushing twin prams, eyes widened at the sight of two more beautiful babies nestled within.

In the end, it was not the judgments of others that defined us but the love that bound us as a family. We were a testament to the power of acceptance, choosing to forge our path rather than succumbing to societal expectations. And so our story continued a tale of love and resilience, proving that in the end, love always wins.

Jane and Yuli, my two extraordinary wives, had each brought a new life into the world. A baby boy named Ken, born from Jane, and a baby girl named Celeste, born from Yuli, completed our ever-growing family. Daddy marveled at the joyous chaos that now enveloped our household, where love knew no bounds. Our two eldest children reveled in their newfound roles as not just siblings but protectors and guides to their younger brother and sister.

Our days were filled with laughter, tears, and endless endearment. I often found myself pausing, taking in the sight of my extraordinary family, and feeling an overwhelming sense of gratitude. I consider myself the luckiest man to have ever walked upon this great planet Earth.

And so, our journey continued, with each passing day cementing the bonds that connected us all. Our home overflowed with love, a sanctuary which acceptance and open-mindedness reign supreme. Together, we navigated the highs and lows of life, finding contentment in the knowledge that we had each other.

THE END